THE OTHER CITIZEN

For St Mary
the Virgin

THE OTHER CITIZEN

BRUSH OULAI

BROWN
DOG
BOOKS

Published under licence by Brown Dog Books and
The Self-Publishing Partnership Ltd, 10b Greenway Farm, Bath Rd,
Wick, nr. Bath BS30 5RL

www.selfpublishingpartnership.co.uk

ISBN printed book: 978-1-83952-448-6
ISBN e-book: 978-1-83952-449-3

Cover design by Kevin Rylands
Internal design by Andrew Easton

Printed and bound in the UK

This book is printed on FSC certified paper

MIX
Paper from
responsible sources
FSC® C013604
FSC
www.fsc.org

ACKNOWLEDGEMENTS

It is undeniable that a series of national lockdowns during the COVID-19 pandemic has brought about a sense of fear and anxiety around the globe. Since the phenomenon was affecting young as well as adults, psychosocially and mentally, I thought it could be helpful to weave stories that uplift people's souls and minds to defeat the virus rather than surrender to it. *The Other Citizen* is a narrative to override the magnitude of the impact of COVID-19 on many vulnerable in our society.

This book would not have been possible without the support of my family. I am indeed indebted to Rose, my wife, for allowing me to taste the creative world. Many thanks to my lovely girls, Taddy and Deslay, who read my numerous drafts and helped make some sense out of the confusion. My endless gratitude to my dear friend Jean Thompson for proofreading the manuscript. Her suggestions and passion to raise the standard of my works have been a real catalyst and confidence builder for my adventure. Thank you to my loyal friends Alan and Eileen Wiltcher for their encouraging words and thoughtful feedback, which reshaped this book. I also thank the many that contributed to the making of this book through their personal experience of life in detention. And finally, my gratitude to the children, Anaiah and Moriah, who wrote to the Ministry of Immigration, a service they have no knowledge of. I bless the Lord our God for inspiring me and giving me a long life and good health.

While I was putting my notes together, the storyline moved from the actual events to a kind of fantasy and fiction, with its own tale. Thus, the more I put my thoughts together, the more excited I became. I felt like pouring more stories. But a book must end. The experience of writing this book has sharpened my appetite for writing. I am currently working on a second book, 'The Killer of Politicians', a pure fiction. I can't wait to publish this thriller.

CHAPTER 1

Land of opulence and conviviality, Kombi is an exemplification of success and political ingenuity in a neighbourhood well-known for coup d'états and larcenies. Kombi is the fruition of one man's vision, its funder, and architect of governance by concession. The coastal land of Kombi, which stretches from Cape Palmas to Cape Three Points, commanded respect from its neighbours for its early success until the pathetic coup d'état by General Zetouma to refrain the dominance of the country's political landscape by one ethnic group. However, his administration died prematurely, lasting a mere thirty days on the calendar. Yet the population continues to pay the price for his actions; nepotism, bigotry, and all forms of malpractice cropped up overnight allowing government officials to substitute themselves to lords and deities.

The weather in Kombi presents a sharp contrast; the North suffers from arid winds, high temperatures and a fauna lamentably dominated by savannah and grassland. The eastern region enjoys a mild temperature favoured by rainforests. The great western province is the "spoilt child". It is always mild in the West and some parts can register five degrees on the Mercury. Occasionally, the temperature drops to minus one-degree Celsius. The West benefits from forests, mountainous highlands, immense river systems, and a gigantic rift of valleys. The view of high mountains bordering deep valleys in the West is astonishing, large columns of trees dominate the littoral. A particular mount on the border of Kombi and Maputa owns strange animals; toads that do not lay eggs but give birth to their smalls.

It's early June in Kombi and all eyes and minds are fixed on adventure and family reunion for those in cities. Summer vacation is the time of the year wealthy families and especially politicians show the class difference by travelling as far as possible from the continent.

Ahead of the school break, children from wealthy families turn their conversation to their next adventure, what's on the cards for exploration; they wonder whether the choice of destination by their parents will meet their expectations this time. Occasionally, they criticise their parents for selecting countries they judge as unattractive. They admit their parents' choice of holidays is heavily influenced by their desire to rediscover countries they visited in their youth or to brush up on their foreign language skills. Thus, they assume they should be consulted on holiday destinations. They baselessly believe they know better than their parents as they do some research ahead or pick their friends' brains for inspiration. In most cases, children prefer popular destinations and especially major cities, while some parents would rather visit historic sites. 'I don't want to learn a foreign language or see a concentration camp; I am not interested,' they moan. 'I just want to enjoy myself and spend time in places like New York.' Omitting the fact that the children of wealthy politicians and some rare businessmen are dropped off every morning and picked up at the end of the day in executive cars, they are unmistakably recognisable not only by their posh accents but the substance of their daily conversations. They chatter about countries they have visited, where they will be going next year, the must-see or perfect holiday destination and, of course, girls. Poor children talk about girls too, but they generally do not speak out lest they are scorned. They cannot treat girls; hence they keep their feelings to themselves.

Summer vacation has another connotation for the Africans; it is the time the Bengis (the Africans that live in Europe), the football stars and musicians emerge from their hiding places. The Bengis are recognisable by their outlandish haircuts, their outfits and how they talk. They behave differently. While some are delighted to be at home, others look confused and apprehensive. They drive foreign registered cars that are typically sold as bargains towards the end of their stay. Some people thirst for those holiday cars; they are clean, well serviced, and eye-catching. JT envies the Bengis; he believes they live a life full to the brim and hopes to be able to equal them when he has completed his education. He'd love to taste such an abundant life.

For the children of farmers and the less privileged in society, there is one option: family reunion in rural areas. As thrilling as the end of the school year could be for students, the month of June is a challenging period of the year in the farming world.

This is the time when forests intermittently discharge dark smoke in the air in the late afternoon as farmers continue to clear lands for sowing. It is also the time of the year many rural roads become two parallel lines, the mark of car tyres. Between these two lines lay a band of grass where dangerous insects and snakes rest and strike anything that crosses those lines. In June, the lines become thin and broken in many places due to the irregularity of vehicles. Weekly markets lose their enthusiasm as farmers run out of produce to supply the market. Similarly, merchants from nearby towns restrain their trips to remote villages due to poor sales since most villagers can no longer afford anything.

Unfortunately, this is a time farmers cannot rely on nature either. Yet, their freezers and storage are empty. The storage is the farm. But June to July is a weird period when all seems to disappoint. Sporadic rains mean that the snails cannot come out yet, they need constant rain and a wet environment to travel easily on dead leaves. Tortoises cannot come out either because their favourite mushrooms have not sprung out yet. Snails and tortoises and mushrooms are the main ingredients of a good source that mothers prepare in rural areas in times of scarcity. Some mothers send out their girls to fetch those ingredients while they venture in light forests for cassava roots or other edible tubes for the day. Men impatiently await heavy rains for brooks that surrender their farm to be filled with water and brink fish. Worse, there are no bananas either nor fruits except for the late mangoes that attract mosquitos.

There is nothing to celebrate in the rainy season bar the football tournament that breaks emptiness in rural areas.

It is against this backdrop that JT and Tcheba approach this summer holiday. As Tcheba packs his latest designer clothes, he ponders on the living conditions in the village. He's not a regular village summer vacationer. His last experience was unpleasant, and he is nervous this time around. Nights were unbearable, the infamous bloodsuckers and noisy mosquitos never failed to feast on them. Worse, the lack of streets lights in the village condemns young and adults to abide by early and awfully long nights. It is difficult to circulate in the village without a torch after 7pm. The streets, if one can call them that, are neither straight nor wide in some places. They are, in fact, paths between houses, and their width and practicality in the rainy season depend on footfall between neighbours. People collide at night as cars do in poor visibility. Thus, doors close at 8pm and open again from 6am at the break of dawn. The village becomes a ghost town after 8 am as farmers return to their respective farms. The routine repeats without fail seven days a week, and its monotony made the three months of holiday feel like forever in the mind of Tcheba.

Tcheba's lowest point in the village comes at night. He does not step outside at night for fear of coming across snakes. He can't set his eyes on anything that crawls as he can't distinguish between what bites and what does not. He is nevertheless aware that some young people in the village will be excited to hear that he will be among them soon. They like him for his attitude towards life; he always dresses up well and his football skills are a wonder to watch. They know that he will bring with him some footballs, as well as kits, for them to train for the upcoming tournament. The village football team thrives through his contribution. Many young people in the village would like to go to school to be able to afford designer clothes like their role model. They also enjoy listening to him; he struggles with his mother tongue. Others encourage him to speak properly. 'This is our language. How are you going to teach your children lest you plan to lose your culture?'

JT has his own experience of endless nights too. That night, JT woke up to an intruder. He usually stays in the farmhouse after a long day because the road to the village is too risky at night. Five brooks stand on his way to the village, which is only thirty minutes' walk from the farm. Three of the brooks only come into existence between June and December, and one of them extends over 500 metres in width. They are crossable by foot; however, JT abhors the fact that he must each time remove his trousers when he reaches them. The water can reach his chest at one point. JT is aware that, in time of flooding, snakes lurk on water edge in the search for food and the thoughts of a snake invasion makes night trips scary and more dangerous. Thus, on that night, JT could not believe his eyes. A black snake was struggling to exit the property having swallowed some mice in the loft of the house. It was moving dangerously, travelling between the ceiling and the wall. At each corner it comes down, hoping to locate the gap it used to enter the house. When unsuccessful, it moves up again with its tail dangling near the floor. It finally located the porous bamboo stash door and vanished. But the time the snake spent moving up and down with the tail about a metre away from JT's head was agonising. JT stopped breathing to avoid attracting the beast's attention. He knew the snake would defend itself if it were in danger. He wondered if he should behave like a man and strike the snake or let it go in peace. He concluded that it would be unwise -and taking a big risk -to try and kill the snake in the absence of a machete or a strong stick since his mother was asleep on the other side of the room. JT could not sleep again until daybreak.

On the second day of the school holiday, the two friends decided to hit the road for the village. JT guesses what his mother may cook on the first day. He misses the region's delicacy; he has not tasted his favourite okra sauce with smoked fish since the end of the Easter holiday. 'I'm sure Mum must have saved some smoked fish to treat me when she sees me. Although she may not know exactly the day I'll be back, I think she'll have a vague idea. She'll be expecting me any time between now and the beginning of next week, I suppose. I wonder how far she may have gone with sowing the rice seeds. I'll be a great helping hand at this time of the year, so she'll be beaming when she sees me. I will get some farming tools here; they are not overly expensive. I know Mum will be using the same tools she has had for the past three years. The trouble is, how do I get in touch with her and find out what she needs with no telephone nor direct postal service in the village?'

'How long to go, JT?' asks Tcheba as he checks the time on his fake Rolex watch.

'I'm almost done, brother,' responds JT in a rather surprised voice; he was daydreaming. 'I'm just looking for a book,' he adds.

'Which book?' Tcheba asks.

'A math books.'

'Are you kidding me? This is only the second day into the summer holiday, and you are talking about books again, is it all well with you?'

'Yes, I just want to ensure that I have everything I need to prepare for next year.'

'Look, I don't want to miss the coach. You know well that coaches only go to the village once a week. If we miss our connecting coach, we will have the choice of wasting seven precious days with Uncle in Deen or trekking forty-five kilometres of road. Unless we take a risk and get off at the junction in Flan. But if "DU Destin" comes full, we will have eighteen kilometres to cover by foot. Would you prefer that? We need to leave Mano at two pm latest to catch "DU Destin" at five pm in Deen for the village. Don't you want to see your Mum today?' Tcheba asks, hoping this will make JT speed up.

'Ok, fine!' he says as he picks up the pace. 'Have you seen my yellow copybook somewhere here in the room?'

'Copybooks? Are you alright? Listen, meet me on the road. Why didn't you organise all this beforehand? What were you doing yesterday? You are wasting vital time, I'm gone. I cannot wait any longer. I know Antuwa is at the coach station already. The first coach from Seg reaches Mano at about two pm in light traffic. I'm sure Antuwa will be on the first coach from Seg. Knowing her, she would rather get off at Flan for a thirty-minute march to her village. I do not see her taking the chance of going to Deen for a connection. If we do not get on the same coach, that is. I will not be able to see her over the summer vacation. You know that she would rather stay with her parents in the farmhouse outside the village. And you are also aware that we won't be welcome in the farmhouse. Her parents won't allow this to happen, no way. I don't want to face a barrage of questions.'

'Okay, why don't you go and tell the driver that you have some friends on their way? You know that they cannot leave without filling all the seats, and sometimes they add extra seats to make the most of their trip, extra seats for extra money that will be used to bribe road controllers. If the driver knows that more passengers are on their way, he will delay the departure.'

'Okay, understood! See you shortly.'

Tcheba made his way to the coach station hoping to meet Antuwa. He swiftly moves to the first coach stand. 'Excuse me please, has the first bus from Seg arrived yet?' he asks a station attendant.

'Yes, about an hour ago.'

'Did you see a young girl of dark complexion, big eyes and long dark hair coming off the bus?' Tcheba inquires, hoping that the answer will be yes.

'I have no idea who that lovely girl maybe. There are many young girls who go through this coach station every day, so I do not pay attention to any young girl whether dark or fair-skinned anymore. Sorry to disappoint you, young man.'

'Okay, thank you,' murmurs Tcheba as he moves on to the next attendant. But the attendant was busy getting passengers for the few empty seats remaining. 'Excuse me, sir.' The attendant brushes Tcheba away, more interested in the customer in front of him with huge luggage (extra bags carry extra money).

'Sang, Madam?' he asks.

'Yes,' she replies with a smile. 'I hope you will do me a favour, sir.'

'Sure, today it's only six hundred CBEE for you, Madam.'

'What? Isn't four hundred CBEE anymore?'

'Correct, usually it is but this is the summer vacation period, and we are overwhelmed by the demand for transportation. You know it normally costs two hundred CBEE for the baggage alone, but I did not charge extra for this.' He was lying.

'Please do me a favour, I am a student.'

'Okay, five hundred CBEE.'

'Okay, thank you, sir.'

Tcheba becomes exasperated. He tries his luck with another attendant.

'Does she wear glasses?' the attendant asks.

'Yes, yes,' Tcheba replies, nodding in anticipation.

'Well, a girl matching your description bought a ticket with me a while ago. Beautiful girl, *hein*. She looks like a model.'

'That is right. Where may I find her?'

'Over there,' he points. 'That blue coach at the petrol station. Hurry, the coach is already full and ready to depart.'

'Thank you, sir.'

'Good luck!'

A muddy red coach from Bey Lato, a town near the Maputa border, moves into a parking bay in front of Tcheba, forcing him to stop. Fellow drivers cheer him as a hero. He must be immensely popular!

'How is the general?' a driver enquires, referring to the head of state of Maputa, a neighbouring country.

'The general is doing well,' replies the man with a rather cynical laugh. 'He sent his greetings. He may visit us soon, his office said.' They all laugh a loud laugh. They knew the man was joking; who are they to receive the visit of a head of state unless he comes to take them away and jail them for criticising him? To avoid repression from some brutal dictators, people tend to give them a nickname. But Tcheba was not interested in their conversation. He moves away and darts through the packed crowd of passengers and hastily passes a taxi dropping off some passengers to only be held back by an uncle who had not seen him over two years. 'Look at you now, big boy *hein*? How is school?' Tcheba, now paralysed with the possibility of missing the blue coach, could only respond with a nod of his head.

'Is it well with you, son?' asks the uncle.

'Oh yes, papa,' Tcheba replies indifferently. 'Sorry Uncle, let me give a note to my friend on that blue bus over there.'

'By all means.'

The indicator of the blue coach was already on by the time Tcheba bolted across the road to reach the petrol station on the other side of the coach station. The driver blew his horn in anger and yells at Tcheba. 'Can't you watch out before you cross the road or do you want to cause me a problem!' He burns his tyres as he zooms out the station like a motor racer, giving no chance for Tcheba to look inside the coach. 'Stupid driver,' Tcheba says in anger. He knew that he has unquestionably missed Antuwa. Defeated, he spun around and directed his anger at JT, who was leisurely dragging an old red sports bag towards him, and some stuff wrapped in an old newspaper inside a large plastic bag. 'It is all your fault JT! That is why I was urging you to hurry up. Do you see what you have done to me? You spoiled my summer holiday.'

'You missed Antuwa?'

'What did you expect?'

'But you came long ago, did you go somewhere else first?'

'Don't get to my nerves! You delayed me then this old coach driver wasted my time.'

'How disappointing! Never mind! Who knows, there may be some opportunities ahead? Think about the joy of being with the family tonight. I'm sure she will find a way of getting in touch with you, trust me, brother.'

'Du Destin' was popular on the road from Deen City to Dag for the unmissable musical blowing of the horn of his twenty-two-seat minibus. No one knows how he presses the horn of his countryside bus to produce such a distinguishable song; it is a kind of music intro. At half-past 6pm on the clock, a couple of houses appear at the end of a narrow road. The visibility is still clear and JT and Tcheba could see smoke coming out the top roofs of houses almost stacked together in most cases. Some women are still cooking the evening meal. DU Destin blows his horn to alert the village of his presence as he always does. Curious children stick their necks out and some run to the coach as if they were expecting someone. Not much to see for Tcheba; giant trees surrounding the village and a small open area wide enough to park one or two cars. The only decent house in the village stands next to the parking space, and it is Tcheba's family house. Aside from Tcheba's family house and three further in the centre of the village, which is covered with metal, all the so-called houses in the village have their roofs covered with palm leaves. JT must walk around three clusters of houses to reach his mum in a small, round house at the end of the village. Inside the house, two wooden chairs and a small do-it-yourself bed. The bed frame is made of bamboo and the mattress is a local material consisting of a variety of cords and lianas smoothed by matching. The lamp in the main room projects a poor light since it has its glass broken in places and supported with some paper to prolong its lifespan.

There was cheering as Tcheba stepped out the coach. 'He is here, Tcheba is here,' someone shouted. And within seconds the small place became crowded. The joy that this summer football tournament will be a success for the village could be read on the faces of the youths who came to greet him. 'We'll win our third trophy this year. I heard Baby Dean is not coming for this trophy. It seems that he has some exams in September this year,' one of the players was commenting. 'Baby Dean destroyed our chance of winning our third trophy last year, but this time we have Tcheba. We have our hero, but last year's winner is without their talisman.'

'Are you sure that Baby Dean will not appear at the last minute? He may just come for the tournament. So don't jinx it yet,' another player warns.

Unlike JT, Tcheba knows nothing about farming and what

it takes to bring food to the table in the village. His father has many contractors and never encouraged his son to work on the farm, he does not need his help. So, for him, summer means more time for football. JT received rather a different welcoming as a future for the village. He has his followers too. Many young people in the village aspire to leadership and JT is the man they look up to. They believe his hard work will introduce him to high places in the country. He incarnates hard work, dedication, and hope for the hopeless. He always encourages young people to be focused and raise their expectations. He believes that nothing is impossible provided they put their mind to it.

Tcheba could not wait for the highlight of the summer holiday, the football tournament since he narrowly missed Antuwa at the coach station. If he could, he would bring forward the date for the tournament. It is a perfect platform for a potential reunion with Antuwa. Tcheba has his eyes on the game in her village. 'Even if she does not like football, she will not miss the quarter-final match in her village. This is the only event for this summer and not attending will amount to a missed opportunity to meet some friends after almost two months. Hopefully, she will be among the spectators. I must perform well on the day to draw her attention. God willing, I will score, why not? Am I not currently the leading goal scorer?' he was hoping.

When it comes to football, Tcheba is a genius. He can score spectacular goals in tight angles and especially with his left foot. He can score in any position. He loves seeing the surprised looks on defenders' faces when he pulls off the bicycle kick. His prayers were that it would not rain on the day so that he could display his talents. A wet pitch not only limits movements and speed but also makes the football heavy and slippery.

Antuwa was excited to see Tcheba after the match. 'Are you returning tonight or staying over?' she asks with a smile that brightens his face.

'I don't know yet. It's up to our coach,' he replies while wiping the beads of sweat from his forehead.

'What do you mean, it is up to the coach, can you not decide for yourself?' she asks.

'Well, generally after a football match we return together. It does not mean that no one can negotiate a sleepover. It happens occasionally.' Tcheba was hoping that Antuwa will ask him to sleep over. 'Maybe romance is on the cards for Antuwa and I.' People always thought that they were boyfriend and girlfriend, but she has never given him the chance to talk about romance. Before Tcheba could veer the conversation in that direction, she innocently moved the conversation to the end of year results and the excitement of reaching the final year of sixth form. She was rather keen on talking about the future and the year ahead like JT.

'How did it go this year,' she asks.

'Not too bad,' he replies unconvincingly. 'And you?'

'Well, it went really well, I topped my year group. How is your bookworm friend?' she asks excitedly, referring to JT.

'He is alright. You know him, he is helping his mother with farming.'

'I admire that man; I mean I like the fact he always helps his mother with farming. I'm also helping my mum with weeding out in our rice farm.'

'Are you? You know how to do it?' Tcheba asks with amazement.

'It's not rocket science. All you do is separate weeds from rice, but it's tedious. You bend for hours while insects bite you. However, our work is done in a group, it's enjoyable in that sense. It's rewarding too, this means the rice plants will grow free and produce grains in abundance. Above all, it is also a great opportunity to spend more time with my childhood friends. You guys are lucky to be with your juvenile friends in town. As the only girl from my village to be in school, I do not have that luxury. Hence working together gives me the rare opportunity to catch up. I understand you don't do any farming work, lucky you. Will you extend my regards to JT?'

'I will,' he says, with the apparent jealousy in his voice. 'So, when are you going to visit us?'

'You know that my parents will never allow me to visit men unless you want to get me in trouble?'

'Perhaps, you could you tell them that you would like to spend some time with your aunty?' (Antuwa's aunt lives in Tcheba's village.)

'Here she is, Waza is looking for you,' a teenager abruptly interrupts their conversation.

'I will be right back, Tcheba,' she says reassuringly as she is whisked away.

'No wonder she admires my friend,' Tcheba was thinking.

'They share many passions; studies, farming ... what else? And what is the point of talking about school results at the end of a football match? Does she want to impress me or embarrass me? What if I had failed my year? I felt like I was being scrutinised by a parent. I had to choose my words carefully. Her eyes seemed to be seeking the veracity of my words, which was intimidating. She only said "well done" for the superb goals I scored to qualify my team for the semis, but the praise was short-lived. Does she want to know that I am also brilliant at school? I am only an average student. I cannot spend hours and hours studying like JT. Perhaps she was hoping to see him at the tournament, not me.'

Waza was one of the first students in the region to lead off to higher education. Law student Waza commands respect in the neighbourhood. Not only was he a brilliant student, but he was also popular in the region for his stance on girls' right to education. Many parents favour their first-born male for schooling. They did not believe girls could make it in academia and therefore did not want to waste their little cash on books and school uniforms in vain. He knew this well and wanted to change parents' perception of girls' education. Girls are equally as intelligent as boys, but they often fail to complete their education. And this striking truth supports some parents' attitudes: high prevalence of premature pregnancy among schoolgirls. Away from parental control, many girls become the prey of paedophiles in teachers' disguises. Some teachers abuse their position and coerce girls or lure them with the weapon of favour and good marks. Waza was powerless when it comes to teachers' punishment for delaying and undermining girls' futures in the country. He concentrated his effort on encouraging schoolgirls; he knew all the girls who were studying in secondary schools in the area. Each summer, he meets with them to motivate them and ensure they are coping. He sometimes meets with their parents to thank them for giving a chance to their daughters. He assures them that like the boys, their daughters could also help them when they make it in life. 'Office work does not require physical strength; men and women are equal in that sense when it comes to performance,' he preached.

He had a short conversation with Antuwa, which Tcheba worried kept the pair too close. They were laughing, touching each other's shoulders, and holding hands. Antuwa was also popular for her dedication to education. Unlike some girls who easily give in and rely on male support, she counts on her own abilities. She does not like favours that would undermine her own efforts. She is a proud young girl who takes full ownership of her own achievements. But Tcheba has another interpretation of their chat. He finds that the conversation lasts rather too long. Worse, she did not return as promised. It was getting dark, and she decided to join her parents at the farmhouse after the football match. Excited to have met Waza, her mind went straight to next year and forgot that Tcheba was still waiting for her. She knows that Waza will ask for her results again next summer. She was already mentally planning for the year to come. Bitterness resulting from frustration and a sense of belittling came over Tcheba. He felt humiliated by the way Antuwa had treated him. He believed his social status may have contributed to this.

JT was curious to hear about Tcheba and Antuwa's encounter the following night, but Tcheba decided to hide the negative side of it. 'She was excited to see me, but her parents forced her to return to the farmhouse.' He was lying to hide the affront he felt on the night. He knew that JT would make fun of him if he told him the truth.

'What a shame, is there anything else that I need to know?' JT asks. 'I mean, did you try to invite her? You should have. By the way, well done. Two games to go for the trophy?'

'Yes, my friend. You need to come and support us.'

'Sure! Was Waza there?'

'That man? I thought he was a good man.' He could not rein in his anger. He must let it go, and maybe JT is the right person to hear his side of the story and bring judgement.

'What do you mean?'

'Uh … no, I am not sure he is really campaigning for girls' education in our region. Don't you think that he has a hidden agenda?'

'Don't be silly!'

'Well, your "Waza" sent a boy to call Antuwa while we were still talking, and she did not return. I do not know what he told her.'

JT couldn't help himself, he first belly-laughed then exploded with a loud laugh. 'Now I understand. Listen, you better get yourself together and apologise to Waza if you said anything stupid. You would not have known her had it not been for Waza. He chats with these girls just to encourage them.

Don't you know that he has a fiancé? Waza is a gentleman that I admire. Please, have respect for this man. He is one of the rare breeds in this area that fight for education. You do not know the bad ones. I reserve the right to seal my mouth about the bad apples you naïvely follow, those who never help you nor direct you. Those who will be happy to see you drop out. Be very careful, I know what I'm talking about. With time, you will understand. Are you looking forward to next year? I think you should. Very soon we will enter the university and command respect like him.'

'I think you are right, brother.'

Tcheba's self-realisation of power and status could be a blessing in disguise. He appears more determined for education to avenge the affront he endured as Waza's envoy disrupted his conversation with Antuwa and any hope for romance.

CHAPTER 2

To JT's surprise, Tcheba was excited about returning to school this time. Tcheba normally prefers the summer break to school time. However, his attitude towards studies have suddenly changed; he vowed to pass his baccalaureate, a passage to university and a step closer to the elite class. He had not recovered from the indignity he was subject to over Antuwa. He learnt a life lesson that evening – power and status. He now wants to prioritise education to be able to sit among the dignitaries. 'To get what I want, I must make it in life,' he huffed. 'I must work hard to get to university to command respect like Waza. If not for his status as a high education student and imminent public servant, would Antuwa run after him and let me wait in vain? We cannot compare, that would be a massive insult to me; big head, big nose, he is nowhere near as handsome as I am. Yet people relate to him and listen to him. They like him for what he represents. He is a role model for many in this part of the county. Even my own friend JT cannot support me when it comes to Waza. The man is from a humble family, not to say poor background. Ha, we cannot compare! My father is the wealthiest man in this area. Honestly, he cannot stand before me and say anything! But his father made education a priority and now people respect his family. The lesson here is simple, people respect those who are ascending, who are doing well. They do not remember the past and for them farming is not a noble profession. They know the history of my family, which means, for now, I can feel comfortable wherever I go. But the reality is, if I am not careful, those from poor backgrounds will soon take over. Now I should take my studies seriously. Soon I will also be at the university and be able to send boys to call girls for me. As a future foreign language teacher, once I enter university, the way I talk, and walk must change. Big man *hein*? He brushed his shoulders, having now consoled himself.

While some children welcome the end of the summer holiday, for many parents, September is an anxious time. Having managed to feed the extra mouths in a time of food scarcity, they must gather the money they do not have for transport, food, and school fees. For those whose children are entering secondary schools, September means a costly trip to cities to look for guardians or a place where their children will stay during school terms.

Although JT is excited about returning to the city, he has never enjoyed the almost four hour-walk to the main road where he can catch a coach to the nearest town. He wishes he could avoid the eighteen kilometres that separate Dag, a village of 150 souls on the border of Kombi and Maputa to the nearest coach stand. Coaches do not reach the village in the rainy season due to road conditions and a slippery mountain on the way. JT and other students returning to school must cover the eighteen kilometres of muddy road by foot. The two-kilometre section of the road leading to the flank of Mount Seiton poses a real challenge. He wonders whether he should use a stick as support this time to make his way up to the top of the mountain. Unfortunately, both his hands were occupied. His mother, a widow, whose only hope is the success of her only son, always packs some rice, okra, smoked fish, cassava, and yam in a bag weighing about 15kg to ensure her son has enough to eat. She trusts that large cities lack the organic foods from the land of her ancestors. While adults can dodge the pressure of small landslides, young people tend to jump over the numerous potholes on the road causing spectacular falls. JT walks painfully behind Sablibli, his uncle. However, he could not believe his luck when his uncle's friend joined them an hour later. The man in his early fifties kindly lifted the load from JT without protocol. JT suddenly felt like a leaf and wondered whether to run or jump to express his relief. He was nevertheless nervous as he did not know when the load would return. He followed his uncle and friend at a reasonable distance. He worried that the man could return his load when he begins to feel the weight. Thus, he kept his distance from both men who were deeply plunged in the past and busy talking about their own time in the city, a little bit of nostalgia. From time to time the pair looked behind to ensure the boy was keeping up with them. But JT's facial expression changes any time the pair check on him; perhaps the man wants to return his load, he thinks. They remembered the great time they had as casual workers for a road construction company in the early sixties in Mano, a charming city surrounded by natural beauty and two large rivers, one to the east and the other to the West. The sky in Mano is always blue and the weather mild unlike other parts of the country. The mercury never goes above thirty degrees Celsius in Mano. In December, the temperature can drop as low as minus one degree Celsius. They talked about their heroic welcome home when they decided to return to the village and take over the farming duty following the passing of their fathers. They were one of the few people who wore decent trousers and appropriate shoes in the village at that time. Neither of them had any qualifications or degrees; they did not even attend school. They could not read or write but managed to find their way. For the uncle, it was a pleasure to revisit the city where he spent a good spell of his time as a young man and a casual worker each September. His friend wishes he had an excuse to visit Mano regularly. He is jealous that his friend is fortunate enough to take his nephew every year to the city they both cherish. He instructed his friend to send his regards to their mutual friends if they were still living in Mano. 'I will make sure I visit all of them this time, I promise,' Sablibli vows. The friend was particularly interested in hearing from a woman who used to sell food near the recruiter's office on the high street. However, Sablibli doubts the woman will still be alive nearly twenty years later. He nevertheless promises to look for her. As they draw near the village of Flan where the major road is, the man returns JT's load. JT was so grateful that they met the man. He did not have much to do now as they were going to catch a coach for the city, a three-hour journey.

September plunges Sablibli into the past. He always looks

forward to a trip to Mano, although it means spending money in a time of scarcity. A week in Mano is a break away from life in the village and a reconnection with the past and old friends. He hopes to meet some former work colleagues before returning to the village. He is going to spend time with one of his old friends who managed to secure a permanent position in the city as a doorman for a wine retailer. The man's job could be described as 'opening the gate in the morning and closing in the evening'. Nothing else he does for the rest of the day. He did not have much to do nor the ambition of moving up as, like JT's uncle, he did not go to school. He counts himself lucky to be an employee and receive a pension when he reaches the retirement age. He is an alcoholic and spends all the little money he earns on women and alcohol. JT has a recollection of his guardian's home time. From the fifth of each month, the man gets home on time since no woman has an interest in him. However, at the end of the month, to say the very first five days of each month, when he has received his wages, he always gets home late as he becomes a source of income for some women that are ready to offer their bodies for some banknotes. His wife, a devoted Christian, never relies on him in any way. She is a businesswoman. Her restaurant serves the region's delicacies to the workforce at a nearby car plant. She also receives a small amount of money for caring for a couple of orphans to supplement her earnings.

While in the city, Sablibli meets the man after work for a glass of wine before they return home together. The two friends fully enjoy the week together. Like the other friend, Sablibli and the man spend their time talking about the past when they were younger. They reunite with two other old friends for a drink. The latter could not get any decent job and were now old and no different from beggars. They did not want to return to their respective village at a time they were still valid for farming. Now old, they regret their decision. Nevertheless, they enjoy being with Sablibli and the other man. They know that each September he will be in town and buy them drinks. However, this September could be the last for him in Mano. This year is the last in high school for JT, and if he does well, which he will, he will be at the university in the capital the following year.

CHAPTER 3

The two friends were fascinated by the sceneries of the capital. They had never seen what was in front of them before. It was tempting not to step out before school resumes. JT passed his baccalaureate with top marks, all A stars, which opened doors to the noble study of medicine, the rule of thumb is only children of wealthy backgrounds are admitted. They are generally the children of politicians and some rare entrepreneurs. JT was exceptionally admitted on merit. His hard work paid off. He bypassed corruption embedded in the educational system where students' career choices are never respected. Family background predetermines access to the faculties that form the elites of the country. For the children of farmers, teaching and other professions are only available regardless of their career aspirations.

Likewise, Tcheba secured a place at the university for modern language studies. The dream to become a language teacher was now possible. Tcheba is gifted with linguistic skills and there is no reason that he cannot do well, except that he may be distracted by life in the fast lane in the capital. He is a man who likes showing off, he always wants to impress people with wealth and abundance. The reality is, that Gadu is where you meet people who are wildly rich and blindly arrogant. He may soon realise that studies at university are different from what he is accustomed to. Still, Waza will be a constant reminder for him to focus on his studies. The possibility of winning Antuwa's heart as a university student with a job almost guaranteed could be the core motivator for Tcheba. Failure to qualify as a teacher will certainly mean losing Antuwa.

No one can master the streets of Gadu, the capital of Kombi, without a taste of the central coach station. The city lies on the south-eastern coast of the country. Home to 2.5 million people, Gadu is the main destination for economic migrants from the neighbouring countries. The city, like most colonial towns in Africa, is laid out on a grid plan. There are large and extravagant villas, residential homes for wealthy locals as well as expatriates and foreign diplomats. Wide and shady streets and gardened squares are the norms in those areas. The only university and the pride of the country is in the east of the capital. The city centre displays Africa's tallest buildings, headquarters to most international organisations. Some parts of the city are the photocopies of some Western cities. Large multinationals boast their logos on large boards or flags on those skyscrapers. Security and safety are guaranteed in and around the city centre. Men in uniforms are visible on every single corner of the commercial district to assure the security of citizens and property alike. On the other hand, the city's older buildings are found in the most densely populated residential areas. Noise, - dust, insalubrity, robbery, and violence are the norms in those areas that accommodate drug dens. MLN, the main drug den, closes the south-eastern entrance to the central coach station. Obscure streets emerge at the first roundabout that dispatches coaches to various international routes. Gadu is the city of lights for tourists who have never discovered the other side of the capital. For the locals, life in Gadu mirrors life in the jungle; only the strong survive. The weak celebrate their lifelike birds in the air every morning when they welcome the new day as for many, tomorrow has never been a certainty even though they believe the Almighty God will protect their lives. Criminal gangs lurk around the international coach station to steal, harm, and kill. The inhabitants of Gadu know well which areas to avoid whether day or night. They can all read the writing on the wall. Whoever has crossed the station has his untold thriller story and now it was time for JT and Tcheba; the new boys in the city couldn't be the exception. Although the two inseparable friends had lived in one of the largest cities in the country and had some experience of roughness that presents cosmopolitan agglomerations, life in the capital was something they had never experienced before. While the boys were excited about life in the capital and the prospect of discovering the city of light, their parents in the village were anxious. They had never seen the capital themselves but news from the city has never been good news. People get killed or robbed. Living conditions are harsh. People live in crowded accommodation and food is scarce. On the other hand, Gadu is where money is made, and home to the wealthy and politicians. It is the capital that dictates all things in the country; in that sense going to the capital brings hope. JT and Tcheba set out on their touring project. The boys gather all their little cash for a shopping spree and a visit to a relative in 'MLN'. The visit to the relative requires them to pass through the international coach station. There is no landmark, nor proper stand numbers at the coach station. Travellers follow diverse slogans written on the front of coaches as best indicators for destinations. 'Discover Aksumite', 'Sun of Maputa', 'King Cobra', 'Midnight Sun', and 'One Way No Come Back' were some examples of slogans written on the front of vehicles. The city well serves the neighbouring countries in transport. It plays a pivotal role in the subregion.

The pair reaches the coach station in the late afternoon on their way back. They walked past a coach stand, which shows the destination of Wagu, then another one for the far east Aksumite and another one for the direction of far west Maputa, and then they came across a group of poker players. They heard, 'Lottery, win or lose, smile or cry.' JT and Tcheba were curious to see what was going on. They had never played the lottery in their lives before. 'Let us watch these guys play and see how it works,' says Tcheba. It was a basic game; to select a card among three. The magician shuffles the three cards several times and asks the player to identify the card they had previously picked. It is important to note that the cards are laid face up at the beginning of the game. They are clubs, hearts, and spades. The player chooses one of the three and the magician shuffles the cards again, this time the cards face down. If the player identifies his selection, he wins the sum of money he pledges for. If he picks the wrong one, he loses his stake. Tcheba plays for a 100CBEE, which he won easily. He tried again and won 500CBEE. 'There is an easy way of making money in this place, no wonder why people drive big cars in the capital. Why are some people here poor then?' he pondered. He tried one more time for a double. Bad luck, he lost all the money. So, he decided to call it a day, but the organisers encouraged him to try again. 'Lottery, smile or cry,' they say in unison. Tcheba reached for his pocket, but JT hinted not to risk his last banknote. Tcheba believed he had mastered the trick and that the dealer was not that clever. Oof, he lost again! So, with no money left, and in distress, they decided to head toward the third exit, but the bandits told them that they should continue to play. 'We are left with no money now for the game, all we have now is for our taxi,' the pair say.

'Money for a taxi, you must be joking. You must play or else … Do you want to play or not?'

The pair realised they were in danger. 'I will play,' Tcheba says. 'After all, it is best to empty my pockets and save our lives than to refuse and face the consequences.' Tcheba emptied his pockets and turned them inside out to prove it. He looks at the note that read 'Central Bank for Emerging Economies, 200CBEE.' He kissed the last banknote. He looks around to weigh his options. A voice orders him to hurry up. JT warns him not to do anything silly. 'We cannot run,' he warns his friend. He played and lost again. 'Okay now we have got nothing to stake, so we are going.'

'You are what? What about your friend?' they ask.

'Oh no, he does not gamble, he is a religious person,' he says as he shuffled his feet.

'Ask him to lend you some money so that you can make a

big gain, you never know. He may change his mind if he sees "hot" banknotes in your hands.'

'I can't do that. I know him, he will not.'

'Then remove your shirt,' they ordered him.

'This is now serious, what should we do?' They quickly consulted in their language and decided that maybe running was their best option. Perhaps by running, they would alert people at the coach station.

'Ok, I will give you my shirt,' he surrenders.

JT's eyes dart around, behold two men exercising their muscles. They flex their arms and JT could see large veins that looked like lianas surfacing a mass of flesh. They twinkle their eyes. JT became nervous. He quietly put his right hand in his pocket to reach for a banknote and passed it to his friend. Winning was no longer on the agenda. Hopefully, losing again, the bandits would have enough money to let them go in peace. But that was not the case. The bandits believed they were still hiding some money.

'You put our lives at risk,' JT angrily points at his friend.

'You should have warned me.'

'I did but you did not listen to me.'

'You should have insisted. Listen, it is not time to argue. How do we get out of this place is what we should be talking about? Can't you see that these people can harm or kill us?'

'My blood will be upon your head.'

'You will be dead anyway.'

They stop arguing to face reality. 'Please forgive us, we are new in Gadu,' they say.

'Welcome to Gadu, gentlemen!'

Tcheba held his shirt as if he were going to give it to the gang members but instead, the pair rotated their body in a coordinated movement and in a fraction of a second burst through the stack raised by both spectators and gang members. The two men race for their lives at the coach station. 'Help us! Help us! They want to kill us!' the pair scream in a loud voice. They run past the first group of drivers busy dealing with passengers. They seem not to be concerned that much. After all, aggression is nothing new in that place. 'They may be lucky enough to escape unharmed,' some coach drivers say. They do not want to be involved. Each driver has had his own misfortune in the past and prefers to stay away from troubles. They know of the bad boys at the station but were reluctant to report them to authorities. In fact, some have tried in the past and no serious action was taken to deal with gang culture at the station. Therefore, peaceful cohabitation with the gangsters was now on the cards. 'If you don't disturb them, they won't disturb you either. So, let them get on with it, so long as they don't kill the victim.' This was now the drivers' attitude toward the gang culture. The two friends continued their race and reached an area that has some light. At this point, the bandits were concerned that the drivers may close the gate behind them, so they gave up, but collected JT's wallet which they believe contained some cash. This is what they were undoubtedly after. JT did not play, so he must have a lot of money in his wallet. They put their hand on a 500CBEE note and a student ID card. 'The wallet is big for nothing,' they said in disappointment.

C24, the gang leader (C24 was his prison cell reference), has put his hands on a piece of paper that is going to change his life for the better – JT's baccalaureate degree. C24 recently escaped from one of the most notorious prisons in the country, 'Camp 17', located near the border of Kombi and Maputa. The camp accommodates convicts sentenced for life. C24 had burgled the residence of the minister of the interior where his two friends and a member of the minister's family died from wounds sustained during the burglary. 'I did not launch the attack for the sake of stealing but to pour out my anger. Unfortunately, things got out of control, and I became a murderer in the process. I would still have been in the prison had the security guards not lost control of Camp 17.'

As an individual that evaded the prison, there is no future for C24. If apprehended, he will be sent back. Hence, he decided to survive on criminal activities. A thousand thoughts were running through his mind as he observed his ticket to freedom. 'Now that I hold this baccalaureate degree, I believe I can make good use of it; I have an ID and a qualification, which I did not have. I cannot continue with life in "the jungle". This kind of life is what takes many valid men to Camp 17. I was lucky to escape. I can make it in this country if I work hard. There are a multitude of business opportunities here provided you listen to the market. The problem is that we all want to become millionaires overnight. Our authorities lead in the "get rich quick" culture. Our leaders behave like pop stars, they live extravagant lives. Many government ministers are useless. They are only experts in looting without being intimidated.

When I see the type of cars they drive and where they live, it drives me mad. I ask myself if we live on the same planet. The arrogance and the way they treat those who honestly earn their living is despicable. What do they really do for society to deserve wealth and honour? Access to health is not free in the country. Unfortunately, my people honour day robbers, and this encourages the corruption and all sorts of bad governance this country endures. Many people die in the waiting room before they see a physician. Fees must be paid before a sick person sees the face of a businessman in the robe of a physician. What sort of government does not care for its citizens? I witnessed the death of a man in a wheelbarrow at the entrance of a ward in a hospital and this changed me. His parents begged the doctor to save his life first. 'He is the only breadwinner for our family,' the wife said. 'What will we become if he is no more? Do this for the sake of humanity. Save my husband's life, doctor. We will gather money and pay the balance later today.' But the doctor was adamant that they must pay the balance before the man is seen. 'Where do I get the money now? Save his life, he will pay his debt when he is better. Why can't you see him now that we have paid the entrance and examination fees?'

'Madam, you still need to pay for the bed he is going to occupy, the gloves we are going to wear, the use of the toilet etc....' the doctor said. By the time the woman came back with the money, the man had died. From that day on, I turned against those who have the responsibility to help society but abuse their position and make others suffer. 'Hospitals are not private clinics to charge fees for treatment. But the government now demands that everyone pays for entrance and consultation fees on top of their prescription', C24 continues.

'I was not born a criminal, I turned criminal under General KK's regime. It's disturbing to discover that the Ministry of Interior, like that of education and health, have the largest budget. Schools are not free, and excessive enrolment fees push many poor families to withdraw their children from academia. Those who manage to go through the system cannot get a job without corrupting employers. You can possibly buy a school certificate if you have money and can bribe teachers.

With this degree, I can make a difference. Someone must initiate change. My blood pressure goes up every time I come across the so-called politicians that are in fact "licensed robbers" who loot this country. These are the little things that cause tensions to flare up in this country. People have heavy hearts and the moment they have the opportunity; they pour out their anger at the next person that stands in their way.'

C24 knew that he would fail the entry test for the National Police Force. Thus, he bribed the admissions administrator and his name appeared in the national newspaper for the year's intake although he did not sit the test. After two years at the training centre, he qualified as a police sergeant. He was so dedicated, so brutal with criminals that he earned the nickname of 'Finger Byte'. His own force turned against him for his stand on corruption. Some police officers would accept bribery and let criminals go free, but Finger Byte would never do that. Jealousy grew around him, but he paid little attention. He wants to serve his country well, nothing else. He could not report malpractice to anyone since there was no provision to check police conduct in the country. Everyone is preoccupied with money, and they cannot earn enough. Thus, he took matters into his own hands.

Finger Byte went from promotion to promotion. He became Detective JT. He shook apart and exposed criminal lairs. He won the hearts of his bosses. He achieved in two years what they failed to do in ten years. His background helps him too, he gets tip-offs from his old friends. He was always ahead of operations, having received inside information. He leads a special branch of police in Gadu. Police operations became regular at the coach station to the extent that his gang members became suspicious of his fitful appearance among them. He now looks clean and different. But he refuses to disclose his activities to his mates. His only alibi was, that having spent years in Camp 17, he was now feeling tired and sick. But the other gang members remained sceptical about his account given his appearance.

Detective JT continues to visit his former colleagues on occasion. However, the fact that police were intercepting major operations around the coach station raises suspicion over Detective JT's possible involvement. 'Have you guys noticed something? This C24's visit is always followed by police raids. Is he not working with the police?' one of the gang members draws his friends' attention.

'Are you saying that our guy has turned against us? This cannot be true. C24 cannot do that to us. You are suspicious about everything,' another guy argues.

'Well, we will be surprised one day when we all find ourselves in a prison cell,' the suspicious man continues. 'I cannot deceive myself into believing that the old friend who no longer drinks or eats with me is still the same as before. I will do my own homework.'

'You may have a point, "Mongoh" (mate),' intervenes another gang member, backing the suspicious man. 'I have been observing this pattern myself as well.'

Detective JT was fully aware that his rapid ascension in the police ranking and regular praises by his superiors was causing jealousy among his co-workers. Some work colleagues prayed for his downfall and their prayer was answered sooner than they could have possibly envisaged.

One day, the few gang members remaining at the central coach station decided to confront C24 upon his possible involvement in police activities at the coach station. They had heard one of the drivers saying that C24 was a police informant. However, they could not trust the source. But the fact that their major operations continued to fail called for some investigation. They agreed that if C24 was proved to be the informant, he would be punished.

A frantic discussion took place as C24 appeared unexpectedly at the coach station one afternoon. C24 was grilled by his friends on his absence at the coach station and possible change of sides. He struggled to convince his friends that he did not work for the police. The gang members directed their questions to two specific police raids, to which he did not have an answer. He realised that his double life may have been exposed and, a shaky C24 was looking for an exit plan as the gang members pressed to know the truth. C24 knows the rule of the jungle; when you betray the group, you pay the price. There is no exception nor leniency. He knows that if the conversation continues and he confesses, then that would be the end of his days. So, he feigned a severe headache. 'You can go,' they said.

C24 left the place trembling on his feet. He wondered who may have informed his people. 'I'm sure some jealous officers did this to get rid of me. I'm now a danger to the police force. My work is exposing the endemic corruption in the force. Is it not corruption at a high level that granted me entry in the first place? Some officers prefer bribery to correction; they take the money and let the criminals go free. This is not right; this is not what we are supposed to do. We get paid to make our neighbourhood a safe place to live. I will do my best. I will find the person behind this. Thank God, they gave me a chance. I do not think I will come back here again; it would be too risky to come here again since they have cast their doubt on the sincerity of our friendship.' C24 walked past a first coach stand but realised drivers and apprentices alike went quiet at his presence. 'Why do they go silent when they see me? What is happening here? What are they hiding?' He continued to the second coach stand and again, the same silence. As he walked past the third stand, behold, four men appeared, all with face masks. He tried to avoid them by turning right, two men armed with knives stood, eyes fixed in his direction. He took a left and about three metres away, a further three men he barely recognised were looking in his direction. Before he could scream for help, the circle closed in on him. Coldly, they ended his life and abandoned his body.

The national press was quick to announce the death of Detective JT. Tributes flooded in for a brave officer who had arrested hundreds of criminals in the most dangerous parts of the capital's slums and drug dens. 'Detective JT, well known as "Finger Byte", our hero, has been killed by bandits in broad daylight,' the news read. 'We vow to leave no stone unturned. There is a one million CBEE award for anyone that has a credible source of information,' the spokesman added. The minister of interior was accused of failing his staff. The budget for inland security has never been fully and adequately deployed. Corruption has led to poor decision-making with deadly consequences.

CHAPTER 4

With the death of Detective JT, the ID fraudster comes the death of JT, the medical student. It was a dark day for the man who had already gone more than halfway through his seven-year course. The fourth-year medical student with a promising future enters a different chapter of his life. He had thought about different ways his ID card could be used, but never did he think it could be used in a high-profile job. His records have now moved to that of the dead. It was the end of the road for a man who had sacrificed pleasure to prepare for a better future. He cannot continue his studies under the same name that is now registered on a death certificate, nor can he change course. The following day, he ran to the faculty's reception to discuss his future. He greeted the receptionist with an apparent anxious voice. She welcomes him with a tempting smile as if she were trying to draw his attention to her excessive makeup before she moves her conversation to students' life cycle on the campus.

'Fourth-year student, right?'

'Yes, I am,' JT replies in an unconvincing voice.

'Aren't you happy that soon it will be over? You guys, from next year, will be on work placement and will be hardly visible on the campus. But your answer sounds like someone who intends to spend their life here on the campus. Is everything all right with you, Dr T?'

'Absolutely, just that my mind slips to yesterday's event.'

'What a tragedy,' she pursues, 'a dedicated police officer, we need just ten or even five of these types of policemen and women in this country and all will be right, security-wise, with us. But he is gone, and I believe none of these officers will have the nerve to confront the gangs that continue to terrorise people in that area. You cannot walk there alone whether day or night. I'm devastated.'

'The police officer who was gunned down yesterday shares my name.'

'You must be proud then. Are you related? Do you know him personally?'

'I don't know him. My concern is that we share the same surname and date and place of birth. How can this be possible?'

'That is weird, is it a mistaken ID?'

'I believe he could be an accomplice to the gang that threatened our lives at the international coach station. Unless the gangsters traded my ID, or he found it himself and did not hand it over to the police and instead used it for his own purpose.'

'Don't be silly, such a good man? How can you say things like that? You will upset many people who praised Detective JT's work not only at the coach station but across the capital. The people who do the job they are paid for in this country are rare, I'm talking about government employees, the so-called civil servants. But this gentleman was an exception. To hear what came from your mouth now sounds like insulting his spirit. I personally think that it's too early to bring up any dirty past. Conduct your own investigation, but if anyone in the high ranking of the police corps hears you making such an allegation, my dear friend, you may find yourself behind bars without trial. You know how things work in this country.'

'I understand, but I fear that the administration of this country believes that I'm dead.'

'Of course, you are not. So, what happened? Did you use his birth certificate?'

'No. Four years back, when I came to enrol at this office, I told you guys that my ID was stolen. I think he could be the person who snatched my wallet at the coach station.'

'No, I do not think so. You need to gather some evidence; you can't just accuse honest people like that. You may land yourself with a lawsuit, be careful.'

'I understand, but it is strange to share the same full name (parent name, village and date of birth) in this country. Just look at his picture, you could tell this man is not from West.'

'You may have a point, but that is not sufficient before the law. How do you demonstrate that just because someone has a long face, he is not from the West? Anyway, I was not here at that time, I only joined this office two years ago. One of you nicked the other's ID to either enter the police training school or the faculty of medicine. The same person cannot be a fourth-year medical studies student and a police officer concurrently, this is not possible. We may be corrupt in this country, but the government does not allow such practice. You cannot nick someone else's ID to make a living. This is a criminal offence. If you snuck his ID to enrol on this course, I am afraid we will have no choice but to remove your records from our database.'

'Do not be ridiculous. Do I look like someone who would nick someone's ID? I am enormously proud of myself. Have I done anything wrong for the past four years here? Why don't you check my records?'

'Do not be upset with me, I am only casting doubt as I do not know the truth or the genesis of the business of ID theft. My apologies if you feel I am accusing you of stealing ID. However, be mindful that the administration of Kombi cannot employ someone who has been declared dead; else you may be prosecuted for fraudulently using the details of a dead person. People can share the same name but not the same parents and place and date of birth. Not even twins share the same full name. So, if that is the case, then consider yourself officially dead. I'm going to make a note on your file and will get in touch soon.'

'What is your advice?'

'Talk to those who establish birth certificates, they can possibly check for you.'

'I will take my case to the police training school.'

'By the way, did you declare your loss to the police?'

'No.'

'Why not, how would someone be sure that you are not trying to steal someone else's ID?'

'What are you insinuating?'

'I'm just warning you that you may find yourself in trouble

with the authorities. You know that the police force is upset about the loss of an officer to a criminal gang.'

The police turn their investigation to JT the student after he claimed that the deceased officer was a criminal. His enquiry at the National Police Training School was perceived as an accusation. The admission office that received JT's request to crosscheck Detective JT's background was furious that JT had cast doubt on their integrity. JT wondered if the police held a copy of the baccalaureate as proof of his qualification.

'Are you inspecting our office?' he asks.

'No, just to compare our certificates since there is a similarity in our name and I believe this can cause a problem for me in the long run.'

'Bring a copy of your baccalaureate certificate, a photo ID of your father to this office within seven days,' JT was ordered.

'Okay thanks, I will do, but I do not have a photo ID for my father, he is deceased.'

'Then bring a death certificate.'

But JT's father died fifteen years ago, and no death certificate was delivered since he died in the village. Looking at one of the admission officer's body language, JT fears that saying he does not have a death certificate may turn things against him. They may think that he does not want his father to come and be scrutinised.

'I will bring it,' he says.

He consulted a lawyer who advised him to drop the case since he did not have a death certificate for his father. Villagers believe it's a waste of time and money to travel to cities to declare that someone is dead.

Without the evidence requested by the police, JT refused to attend the meeting as suggested. Consequently, he received a summons from the police to report to their office within 24 hours. Failing to do so, he will be arrested for a false accusation of authority. They also believe that JT may know something about the death of the officer. Their suspicion grew stronger when JT failed to report to their office within 24 hours. 'Is this man trying to use Detective JT's ID for criminal activities or gauging the integrity of this office? Well, we will find him if he does not turn up.' They visited his flat at the time he was in the library. Two days later, the police knocked on his door, but he refused to answer the door since he was expecting their visit. JT considered changing his address in the capital but there was a possibility of him being arrested on the university campus. Two weeks later, the police visited the faculty of medicine, but there was no trace of JT. Since the lawyer has hinted that the cumulation of no proof to support his case and the fact that he did not declare the loss of his ID could play against him, JT decided to go into hiding. He decided to return to his village until the police eased their manhunt. So, he heads to the village.

The return of JT to the village brings suspicion on his integrity and ethic altogether. Some villagers received the news of JT's return to village life as a loss of opportunity and a big loss for their community. He was nurtured to be the ambassador who could also defend the cause of their village like Waza in the neighbouring village. Sadly, he was now among them and bound to become one of them.

'Has JT dropped out like many others in the village? We are

going to have a bunch of young men who talk like company directors in this village, what is going on?' a man wonders.

'No, he is not a dropout. This man is a "brain". I heard he misbehaved in the city. Apparently, he is on the police wanted list, which is why he ran to the village,' another alleges.

'That cannot be true, this young man is of a good character, we all know him unless you purely want to vilify him,' another man argues.

'Well, you can advocate for the devil, but never trust these new generations. You do not judge a book by its cover. Do you know what takes place in deep waters?' the man defends his claim.

For a minority, the return of JT confirms the existence of social class. He is the son of a poor man and could not possibly become a civil servant and reverse the order in the village; the poor will remain poor. For many, the return of JT is a tragedy. Like Waza, JT was seen as a child who will defend the cause of the villagers. To do so, he must be in a position of power. So, some villagers were thinking about how they could help him return to the city. 'We cannot allow this to happen to us. The neighbouring villages have their intellectuals, and we have none. We must fight to have an intellectual in our village so that they discuss equal to equal over issues that are at our hearts. If we do not have anyone in the capital, who will defend our cause? Look at the state of our road. We do not have anything in this village, not even a water pump,' they moan.

Sometime after JT had settled in the village, mockery, cynicism, and name-calling encircled him. 'How can such an intelligent man be among us as a mere farmer. Well, he will help us lobby the government so that farmers get better treatment. Maybe we should elect him as our leader; village chief,' says one man.

'Have you seen "doctor"? Did this man not say that he will become somebody and help us come out of poverty? Now we are all the same, all poor. They (him and the son of a fisherman) behave like kings in this village. He is the son of a poor man. "Like father, like son" isn't it? I told you that these people cannot make it in life. We will all die in this village in poverty together,' laughs another man.

'Shut your mouth, evil man,' another angrily voices. 'Don't you benefit from the contributions made by the children of this village who are doing well in the capital? Who have you helped in this village? Give me a name. Did anyone stop you from sending your children to school? Is it not your own wickedness that is affecting your children's future? There is a curse upon your head that you should deal with. You should not take pleasure in someone else's misfortune. Will his misfortune change anything in your life?'

'Well said, my dear friend,' another villager intervenes. 'This young man loves and respects the elders. It is a pity that he is among us. We should pray for him to find a way out. So, whosoever mocks this man like this shameful and wicked man over there shall repent. Is it not Waza who lobbied the government for a primary school to be raised in his village? Remember that children from their village used to walk every day three miles to attend classes in the neighbouring village.

Thanks to Waza, their children are spared the long journey. So, we also need someone who will fight for the interest of this village. You see, to get simple medical assistance, we must go to the nearest town, which is forty miles away. Instead of praying for such a man to make it so that it is well with us in this region, you are happy to see him suffer. I guess, as a qualified medical doctor, he would have more power to make the case for a medical centre for this area. You are a wicked man.'

'Well, pray for him, I do not have time to pray for someone else to live a good life while I languish,' retaliates the man. I am happy to have him here. We are all poor and no one can have dominion.' He then left the scene to avoid further attacks, as he realised, he did not have any support.

The mockery was not only behind JT's back; there also was a special song dedicated to him. 'Adventurer' was the title of the song. In that song, singers portray someone who went abroad and came back empty-handed. They didn't explicitly mention JT's name, but through the story, everyone knows that they were talking about a man with a bright future that is now among them. JT recognises himself in the story, but he could not say anything.

JT always argues that no one was born poor, no one was born rich. Only those who discover their God-given talents and develop them become rich. Some musicians are rich, some football players are rich too. He trusts that his talent is in academia, therefore if he focuses on his studies, there will be no reason why he will not make it in life. He grunts at the prospect of dying without redeeming his talent now that he has resumed a life of subsistence. He became so agitated and distressed he cried to God for help. That night he dreamt of an aircraft taking off, a sign of great achievement. 'Remaining in the village will not solve my problem. Man dies once. There must be a way. I need to be in the city; perhaps someone can guide me. Here, the best I can achieve – if I survive the mockery – is farming, and this is the absence of achievement. I cannot just surrender my dream. Dying poor is a human tragedy', he says to himself.

CHAPTER 5

Back in Gadu, JT dedicated his time to church service, hoping that miracles will operate in his life. He joined one of the vibrant churches in the capital, 'The Winners Take It All Church' (TWTIA).

TWTIA is one of the new churches in the capital that teach the words of God. All attendants study the Bible and know Biblical quotes by heart. The pastor, who calls himself 'prophet', claims that his words never go out in vain. His prophecies always come to pass. The church is also known for its healing power; the barren can give birth, the blind can see again, the deaf can hear. The church hosts visiting pastors each month. Crusades are regularly organised towards the end of the year to thank and spread the word of God. Within six months, JT was also quoting the Bible. He could quote the scripture from Genesis to Revelation. He gave his soul and body to the work of God. The prophet was impressed with JT's commitment and progress. He decided that JT should become his assistant. All responsibilities fell into JT's hands; fundraising, prayer meetings, building maintenance, etc. The church grew rapidly in number. However, a time came when the number of weekly attendants began to fall. Disenchantment grew rapidly. 'The church has gone dry,' grumbled some of the church's elders. 'What is going on? Has God forgotten us? Have we sinned? Lord have mercy,' could be heard during and at the end of church service.

Meanwhile, the pastor has a different concern; there is not enough money pouring into the basket. So, he calls in his assistant for some instruction. 'Look, at the end of the month, I want you to make sure that any member of the congregation in a paid job pays you 10% of his salary. Everyone must pay his or her tithe, which is 10% of their earnings according to the Bible. I am not making it up; it is written in the Bible. And you need to organise a special offering section as well. You will get a salary if you do your duty well.'

'Okay, sir.'

JT had such respect for elders that he could not object to his boss's instruction. He holds a record of those who correctly pay their tithes. The Sunday message towards the end of the month always focuses on tithing. The prophet reminds believers about their duties. They must give to the church to advance the work of God. They must donate to the church so that the church can take care of the poor. This is the monthly rhetoric to push people to contribute, but nothing is truly done for the poor. There is no social project run by the church. All money goes to the prophet for personal use.

One day, JT approaches the man he reverently called Uncle and asks for a favour. 'Uncle, you know my situation. Is there any way you could get me out of this country?' His uncle works for the government and has many connections abroad.

'Where do you intend to go?'

'USA, Uncle. I can make it big there, I am positive, trust me.'

'But you know it costs money, what do you have?'

'Nothing.'

'And you want to travel? How are you going to do that?'

'That is why I need your help, Uncle.'

'We shall see.'

'Uncle' is one of the rare people from JT's neighbouring village who had made it to the capital. He is not highly educated but his eloquence and audacity earned him a place in successive governments in Kombi. He worked hard and encourages students from his region. However, he has never been interested in the business of his village. He does not go to the village. He believes the villagers are all wizards and would rather stay away from them. His wife, on the other hand, never supports his vision. She is one of the people blinded by success. She believes she is the boss and can decide who the husband helps. She likes having many young people around her to use as she pleases. The family house, not dissimilar to a five-star hotel, needs maintenance. The woman needs maids, cleaners, gardeners, and drivers. She cannot do it alone and does not want to employ people either. Hence, for the next three years, JT became the driver, head chef and home teacher for his nephews. JT enjoyed being part of the family and being a great support to his uncle. However, time was running out, he was not getting any younger. He thought it could be helpful to hear any feedback from his uncle regarding his trip to the USA. He reckons his uncle has made some progress. 'Any news on my trip, Uncle?' he asks.

'Yes, I am talking to my friend, the transport minister. All is well. I cannot forget. I know this trip is important to you, no doubt about that.' He was lying to his nephew.

At night, JT's uncle discusses the matter with his wife. But she opposes the idea. Her reason is self-centred, she is concerned about her own domestic duties. 'Who will drop and pick the kids from school when your nephew leaves?' she asks. 'Who will assist me with my shopping? Who will look after the house when we go on holiday?'

'Are you saying that he will be with us forever? What happens when he gets married?' the man asks his wife.

'He does not have a job; how can he get married? Which woman would marry a jobless person? Who is going to condemn herself to everlasting poverty?'

'Um, are you saying that only people with jobs get married? Is this why you married me?'

'You know that I love you. I'm not one of those materialistic women who use all means to get wealthy men. Whether poor or rich, I love you. I'm not here for your money.'

'So, why the difference with my nephew?'

'Don't get me wrong,' she was now trying to save her face. 'Maybe, he can stay in the annex and raise his family, but if he leaves us, things will be difficult for us. Remember, it is he who helps the children with their homework. So, think about it,' she adds.

'Okay, that is true. He does not even have money. So how is he going to travel? I will think about what to tell him. It is not easy for my nephew though. He would have been a qualified medical doctor by now had he not lost his ID. I am genuinely concerned about his future. I will see what I can do,' reflects the man.

A stranger hails JT on his way to church. JT crosses Bellard avenue in Zatchi, one of the largest districts in the capital, hoping to talk about God. 'Don't you want to go abroad,' the man asks.

'You must be in spirit,' JT says with excitement. 'Yes, it is my prayer to leave this place one day.'

'Well, your prayer is then answered. Do you have money?'

'Erm, how much?'

'Do you have 2.5M CBEE?'

'No, I do not have such money.'

JT was trying to bargain. Although he is eager to travel, he has a bad memory of what happened to him at the central coach station.

'What would you say if you were given a passport with a six-month visa to the USA? You go as a businessman. The paperwork is clean, done and dusted; five years of trading records in the book. A bank statement is attached to show your company's turnover. You have a business card to confirm your job title. You are the company director on vacation. You have six months to stay legally in the country. However, before the visa expires, you must find a way to remain in the country; get married or work or study. There are plenty of opportunities there, my friend. Those who went two years ago are sending money home already. Some are even building over here. Do you know the "Ethee Estate"?'

'Yes, I go past the estate every time I am coming to church.'

'The estate belongs to one of the guys we sent three years ago. You may also know "the Yellow bloc" near the junction before the market. Another guy from our book is behind that project, they are doing well. So, if you are interested, I will take you to my boss who can answer all your questions.'

'Now you are talking,' JT was thinking. 'Yes, book an appointment for me please.' JT got excited about the prospect of travelling to the USA, his dream destination. 'Over there, I am sure I will make it; if those who went two years ago are building blocks of flats in this country, why can't I do the same? Just give me one year and I will make a name and Mum will be proud of her son again. The wicked man in the village who mocked me will be put to shame. I trust my God. It is not over until I have achieved my goal. Let me organise the funds I need for this trip. Should I inform Uncle? I am not sure because his wife opposes the idea. So maybe I should keep it to myself in case.'

CHAPTER 6

JT's dream turned to reality the day he received a passport with a six-month visitors' visa to the USA. He was so excited that he spent the following two nights without sleep. He was dreaming about what he would do for his mother and the whole village once he is in the USA. Surely, he would make money and set up a business in his homeland like those who had made it. Did the man who linked him with the people who secured his visa not show him the work of their previous clients in Gadu?

'Mr SSF?'

'Yes, sir!'

'Follow us please, we are immigration officers.'

JT follows the two men in a grey khaki uniform. They walk past three desks and slide through a dark metal-framed door. They reach a red desk with a small window at the back. A tiny woman is checking some dodgy passports in the corner.

'How did you get this passport?'

'What do you mean? How do people get passports in this country? You should know, why are you asking me?'

'What do you do for a living?'

'I am a businessman.'

'What is the nature of your business? Describe your business to us. Who are your customers?

'Erm, I mean, we have been trading for some time. You can see our bank statement attached.'

'I know, but that does not answer my question. Looking at you, I can tell you are not a businessman who may have such money in their bank account. We know businessmen in this country by name. You do not fall in that category. You know well this is a fake passport with a fake visa. Have you ever travelled outside this country before?'

'No.'

'I see. What is your real name?'

'It is what is written here. Can you not see it?'

'What's your real name. If this is your real name, then you are going to prison for ten years. We have been looking for this person for some time. He tried to dodge the system for a different destination last year. Is it you?'

'No, officers, it is not me.'

'So, who gave you this passport?'

'I don't know their names.'

'What do you mean you don't know? Are you protecting them?'

'I swear to God, I don't know their names and I don't know where they live either.'

'Well, we are going to keep you here until you tell us the truth unless you want to spend ten years in prison for collaborating with criminals.'

'No, sir, I swear to God, I do not know where they live. We met twice in a public place at an appointed time. So, I do not have a clue where they live. They said they were confident that I will be fine with this passport and that I would not need their help. They said that they would not give me their address. They said it was a risky business, that they did not want their clients to know their address.'

'You will soon know.'

The officers put him in a small dark room and went on their break. They came back two hours later and called him for another interrogation.

'Are you going to give us a name now or not?' they ask.

'Sir, I am an orphan trying to fend for myself. I have tried everything in this country, and no one is prepared to help. I want to try my luck somewhere else. So, these people were like my saviours. I thought I would go through immigration. I did not want to think negatively, so my mind did not go into getting their details. I was focused on making it.'

The officers felt compassionate and believed his account. 'You can go home; this is a favour for you. I normally send people to prison for ID theft. This is a criminal offence and carries at least ten years' imprisonment.'

'Thank you, sir. Can I go now?'

'Yes, you can go. That is how they operate. They know they are in an illegal business and once caught they would be going to prison. Do not worry, we will catch them.'

A dejected JT resumes church service after a week of absence. He wonders if he should give up on his dream or seek other venues. Three months later, he decided to share his experience with a member of the congregation.

'You should have said long ago. You know Ken?'

'Yes, of course, I do.'

'Talk to him. He will help you. You do not need to give him money. He will prepare you for your interview and advise you on where to go. I am sorry for your misfortune but never mind, the good thing is that you are free. You could have been behind bars, and no one would have known, because there is no trial for ID theft.'

'Prophet needs you JT,' a member of the congregation abruptly interrupts their conversation.

'What is this again?' mumbled JT. He wanted to hear more about his new lease of life. He was at church, but his mind was somewhere else; how to leave the country is his priority. He was not interested in tithes or prophecies anymore. How to leave while he is still strong and able is what is in his thoughts nowadays. Anything to do with travelling is his favourite subject. He drags his feet to the office to meet the prophet.

Testimonies are the winning formula used at TWTIA to hook in new members. JT has recently been preoccupied with the preparation of his trip abroad and therefore neglected the work of the pastor, which is to extort congregants' hard-earned money each month in the name of his 'God'.

'What is going on again, my friend?' the prophet queries. 'Our revenue has dropped substantially by more than twenty-five per cent. I want you to get back to work. I need to buy a new car and it is taking too long to raise the money. Secondly, we need more weddings and babies in this place. You may have noticed a hefty drop in the weekly attendance.'

'And you want me to make babies?' he asks ironically.

'No, and yes. I am going to tell the congregation that five bachelors in the church are going to get married within the next six months and five women who have been praying for babies are going to conceive before the end of the year.'

'That is fine by me. If it is what God has shown you, who am I?'

'No, you don't get it.'

'What am I supposed to do?'

'Get five young men you know; they could be your friends or mere acquaintances. You only tell them that you are inviting them to a special programme. I will do the rest. Also, from now on you will follow me in my deliverance prayer meetings. We will pray with those women who are desperately looking for babies. They will have to fast for twenty-one days.'

'You do not mean it, twenty-one days of fasting? Did they kill Jesus Christ?'

'No, but do you think it is easy to get a child? They want children, they must make sacrifices. At the end of the fasting period, they will report to church for special prayers. While we are praying with them, and they fall into a trance, I will need your help as a young man. You know what I mean?'

'No, I do not get it.'

'Well, you, young people want everything in plain writing.'

'You mean I will sleep with them?'

'Uh-huh, you should understand.'

'What? This is called rape. It is also adultery, and I do not see myself doing that, sorry.'

'No, you see, you people "speak grammar". This is not rape. This is called looking after the sheep.'

'I do not think I will be able to look after your sheep; I am not a shepherd. It is an abomination, and we can be punished by God. Even if the husbands of these women were unaware of immoral practice here to ensure miracles flourish, the good God we serve will. What if the women report us to their husbands? This is rape and adultery altogether.' JT began to question the doctrine of TWTIA. 'Are we really serving God? Is this a church? Is it how churches operate? I do not think so. No wonder why it is called "The Winners Takes It All".

'They never say anything. What to tell them is that you act under the direction of the holy spirit. You can say anything in this place provided you invoke the name of God or the Holy Spirit, and especially when you tell them that they are going to have babies, you will be amazed that they will feel rather privileged. You understand that I can do whatever I want in this place and go free.'

'And you are proud to say that?'

'It is not about moral issues here, my friend, we are in business to make money. Money, my friends, easy and clean money. You see, the reason why some of these women are still waiting desperately for their first child is that their men are weak. I know all of them. The women have told me everything during counselling. Why do you think I hold counselling sessions after church service? I know what is going on in every single family that attends this service. Will you help me or not? Do you want to travel? You will get big money through this.

See it as a business. Listen, do you want to help me or not?'

'Let me think about it, sir.'

The whole night, JT could not sleep. 'This is wickedness,' he reflected on the prophet's proposition. 'We are here to teach morality and we should be an example, but to engage in such dirty business is immoral. I cannot be part of this. I think the name of the church gives a clue about its service, but I did not get it in the first place. I came here to find the favour of God, but what is happening here is entirely against His will. Joining this band of evildoers may bring a curse on me and not allow me to travel. What I seek is the presence of God, but instead, I'm moving closer to Satan; it is a dangerous move. How do I get out of this place?'

The following week, JT failed to turn up for church service for the first time since he joined The Winners Take It All church two years ago. The prophet begins to shake. 'Will this man tell people about how I perform miracles here?' he thought aloud. 'I must convince him otherwise he may bring this up in a conversation with his friends. In case he does not react to money, I will blackmail him. He does not have an ID, so the idea of reporting him to the police will make him surrender. He has the choice of engaging in this business or facing the police. He knows that the authorities will trust my word.'

There is a certain time allocated to church announcements and testimonies. A lady emerges from the congregation and picks up the microphone. 'Offering time,' she says.

'Blessing time,' the congregation replies.

'The Lord has done it,' she says. 'Can you not see my finger?'

She shows off a silver engagement ring to the congregation. The scam marriage production line has been given the green light. JT has convinced three men to meet the prophet. They were described the type of women they should marry to make it in life. The men had already heard about the powerful prophet in the district and were convinced that he can only transmit the words of God. Who wants to fail in life? No one. The young men were excited and grateful to have met the prophet, 'a man of God', the one who can predict their future. So, they were happy to join the church. To the women, he prophesied that in a matter of weeks, men would join the church and propose to them.

Three weeks later a second woman stood up. 'Praise the Lord, praise the living God. Our God is good, always good. Souya has proposed to marry me.'

'Hallelujah!' responds the congregation. Keyboard, bass and lead guitars, drums, you name it, anything that can make noise in the church responded to the good news.

'We must now move to the second phase,' hinted the prophet.

Six months later, 'offering time', another woman opens the floor. 'Blessing time,' answers the congregation.

'What can I say unto the Lord, all I can say is thank you, Lord,' sang the woman. Anyone with an ear for music, would know that she was out of tune, but who cares? She just wants to draw people's attention and make a point. 'I am now two months pregnant. The man of God prophesied some time ago and I prayed to God to remember me. The Lord heard my prayer.' A white-large envelope was handed over to the man of God.

Two months later. 'Our God never lies, the man of God said that I would have a child, but I did not believe. Now God has done it! I am now two months pregnant. Praise the Lord, praise the living God,' another woman testified. Another envelope is handed over to the man of God. The news went viral. Every week, new people joined the church. People want miracles, don't they? The church was at its full capacity again and smiles were on the prophet's face. JT could not sleep the whole night. He knew what was going on and his role and responsibilities in the making of the so-called miracles. 'Is it how miracles are performed in this world?' he asks himself. 'Am I going to deny a child of mine? This is not right. For a child not to know his or her biological father is a tragedy. If I claim to be the father, I not only draw problems to myself, but I will break up a marriage. I would have sinned twice. If I say nothing, the child will belong to a father who, in fact, is not his father. How can I tell the child that I am the father? If people discover what we are doing, it would be the end of the pastor and the church. Only God knows what I will endure as an assistant pastor. My travel plans may become an unfulfilled dream. So, what do I do?'

Some weeks later. 'Praise the Lord, God has also favoured me. Pray for me and thank the Lord for me. Our God is faithful.' Another woman appeared on stage with a smile. Some elders in the church looked around in suspicion. 'Don't get me wrong, something fishy is going on here. We need to watch this pastor and his assistant,' reacts Kiebah, one of the elders. He was quickly rebuked by Batin, another elder. 'Why are you so negative? Instead of being happy for these women, you want to know how they get impregnated.'

'Well, if babies are sent by an angel, I would have no problem with that, but if they are the work of the pastor and his assistant, then in my view it would be unacceptable. I am not convinced. So many women are getting pregnant since this gentleman joined this church.'

'That is the point I am making. He is anointed, that is why things are moving here again,' argues Batin. 'Do you believe in God and what He can do? You will have to apologise to the pastor and his assistant, believe me.'

'Well, I cannot wait to see. Babies will come and we will see their faces. I trust science. I have always been suspicious about some women's attitudes toward this young man. They treat him differently. I will wait.'

JT anxiously paid attention to the conversation between the two elders. Although he could not hear anything they said, he could read the body language. His soul was very troubled. 'These elders may cause me problems. I think I need to work on my exit plan. Now that I have a little money, I am going to talk with this brother Ken. The sooner, the better.'

CHAPTER 7

It is one of those afternoons under the tropic when all one can think of is having an ice-cold drink to quench their thirst. The mercury is at 38 degrees Celsius in Gadu, and JT is thinking that since the children are still at school, it could be a great idea to retire under a shade. 'I think the bar near the beach could be the ideal place to be at this time of the day. I hope it has the Kutu drink from the neighbouring country. I would not mind walking down there now. The shop nearby may have the Kutu, but their drink is never cold enough. Worse, there are no seats available for customers wishing to spend some time out. You know what, it may take about half an hour to the beach, but it will be worth the effort. I can stay there until the sun goes down.'

JT praises himself for being at the beach bar. The bar offers high standard facilities that JT was not aware of, including traditional foods in a modern setting. He admires the professionalism of the catering staff. National meals are normally served in informal restaurants in popular residential areas, not in upcoming areas. 'People are having fun in this place while I "count my miseries". I think I may come here from time to time; it was worth coming here. These are the types of things I was dreaming of. That is why I was working hard to make it in life. But look at me now – unemployed with no clear prospect of how things may unfold in future. I may spend my life envying those at the top, which I may never reach.'

'What can I get you, sir?' a bar attendant asks.

'A bottle of Kutu, please.'

'Three hundred fifty CBEE please.'

'I'm sorry?' JT asks in a rather surprised voice.

'Three hundred fifty CBEE, sir.'

'Ah okay.'

'This is a rip-off, this is more than double the price in the corner shop,' JT was thinking. A bottle of Kutu costs 150CBEE in JT's corner shop. However, he did not want to show that he was not a regular customer. People were looking at him already and to bargain the price could make things worse. He spent a few seconds counting his financial losses. 'It is my fault; I could have bought two bottles of Kutu and still have some change had I gone to my corner shop. I can't afford a second bottle with this. I am not sure now whether I will come back here again. This place is for the politicians with deep pockets, not for me. Well, at least I have discovered the place and can also talk about it without mentioning the price of a drink here.'

JT puts his hand on two local newspapers that drew his attention at the reception desk. They both have on their front page the picture of JT's favourite football player. JT read the story of BB Sol's goal of the month. BB Sol is one of the rare sons of the country that is playing professional football in Western Europe. Local papers feature him regularly on their front page. He is a good seller. BB Sol always scores spectacular goals in the final minutes. His club was sitting comfortably in the middle of the league table, but that was not a concern for the people in Kombi; what mattered was BB's scoring. The paper nicely described how he dodged three defenders before slotting the ball in the right top corner and how devastating it was for the opponents that were hoping to share the point. He then flipped through the paper; politics was one of his favourite topics. He updated himself on current affairs. He loves the foreign news column. He was at his second glass of Kutu when he reached the second paper. There were two headlines on the paper: the growing violence on the Northwest border of the country and a church scandal story. 'A church in the capital is under investigation for the conduct of its pastor and assistant,' the local paper read. The paper went on to say that the pastor and his assistant were involved in ritual practice. 'They use the name of God to run a den of iniquity,' the paper quotes. 'The pastor of TWTIA church has refused to speak to our reporters,' the paper continues. 'We are seeking to locate his assistant, who is nowhere to be found.'

'Bloody hell!' JT drops the paper and the glass he had in his left hand.

'Are you okay, sir?' a bar member asks.

'Yes, thanks for asking,' his voice trembled back.

A cleaner was instantly sent in to clear the place, but JT was gone. He even forgot about his change. 'So, reporters are looking for me? I am not going to church tomorrow; I would rather hide. If they get hold of me, my reputation will be tarnished. What shame would that be for Mum? The people of my village will be extremely disappointed in me. What about Uncle? He will throw me out. He will be disillusioned; he trusts me so much that he calls me "the man of integrity". So where has the integrity gone? This is not good for me, my family; I have let everyone down. I must see the brother from the church now. I must leave the country before it is too late. Once the news reaches the church we are done, and the brother may refuse to help me. I must hurry. So, why has the pastor said nothing to me? Does he want to get me in trouble? Who knows, he may turn the attention of the press on me and get away with his dirty business.'

As JT reaches a popular street that will take him to the pastor's house, he overheard a group of young people standing under the shade of acacia trees; 'Is that not the assistant pastor? Surely it is him. These are the people who commit adultery in the name of God. The bible is against some of the practices in that so-called church. Is it really a church? I do not think so.'

'So, what is that business of deliverance anyway?' intervenes another man

'Well, they say that they can cast out demons and chase away some bad spirits from those who are possessed,' suggests another one.

'Well, maybe they should remove "the beam out of their own eye, and then they can see clearly to remove the speck out of their brother's eye," is that not what the Bible teaches us?' quotes another man. 'Do we not know where the demons currently dwell?'

'Of course, we do, unless we want to deceive ourselves,' they reply in one accord. JT heads down with two things in his mind; confront the pastor and then sort out the paperwork for his leave. 'God is great! Gentleman, I was looking for you. What I saw in our local paper today is not good. You must not go to church this week, Kiebah can't wait to confront you,' advises an elder from the church. 'It seems that Suz's husband has banned her from attending our church service. He vows to embarrass the pastor if she insists.'

'Thank you, sir, for your information. I am going to see the pastor.'

'I will let you go. You better do so; your reputation is at stake. Good talk.'

JT heads down again and hopes to meet no one on his way. Unfortunately, five minutes later, when he lifted his head to cross to the next street, he saw a man wearing a red and green shirt. 'It must be Kiebah, he lives nearby. Everyone knows him for his taste for green and red colour.' Kiebah emerged from a local shop with a local paper in hand. He never misses his daily paper, people say. However, it was difficult for JT to identify the one he had in hand since he stood at a reasonable distance. Kiebah looked in his direction, adjusted his hat then headed in the opposite direction. 'Thank goodness, he did not see me. He was not expecting to see me in this area on an ordinary day. After all, I do not blame him, are we doing the right thing? Is silence not complicity in this case? So, let him shake the water to get the fish.' JT is forced to change direction again.

'Hello, man of God. How are you?' JT asks.

'Our God is Great!'

'Are you following the news?'

'No.'

'Well, there are some bad headlines about church conduct in today's paper.'

'I am sure it is in Citizen Times. Don't mind them,' the pastor says. 'I have refused to speak to them. I guess Kiebah must be behind this. He is sceptical about everything I do. He may have his hand in this. But don't you worry, we will win. We worship a living God, the God of the Levant. We are the winners who take all the cream; we are always winners. But what we do not want is the involvement of national papers. If they come, I may be forced to speak. They will not cover this story lightly. So be prepared. Think about what you are going to say. Be strong. Remember, be strong and courageous. Do not shake. If you do, our boat will sink.'

JT heads northward to meet the brother who can help him leave now rather than later when everyone is informed about the scandal.

'Sergeant, can we talk?' JT asks the brother from church.

'Yes, what can I do for the "Man of God"?'

'Please, it is not time for flattery. I am not a 'man of God', Sergeant.'

'Since when did you change titles?'

'Look, this is not a good time for jokes. Is there any chance of talking today?' JT inquires.

'What is the matter that deserves such prompt attention?'

'I will give you details when we meet, can we do it now?'

'Well, it has to be late in the evening, pastor. Probably after 5 pm. I need to finish off what I am doing, sorry.'

'That is fine, provided we meet today.'

'I hope it is all well with you, though.'

'God is in control.'

'Okay, let us meet at the "Allokodrom".' (Allokodrom is a place where some women fry plantain and fish in the late afternoon, from 4pm).

'Perfect, I will be waiting for you.'

The sun had gone down, but it was still bright in that part of Gadu. Fity was busy serving her regular customers, with the usual smile. JT has been waiting for more than an hour; he was two hours early for the appointment. He did not mind the wait of two hours that felt like two days in his mind. He desperately wanted to see Sergeant to discuss the possibility of travelling now. He was so anxious about Sergeant's ability to honour the meeting that he could not sit in the same place. He sits and stands and sits again and stands again as if there was something wrong with his buttocks.

'Sir, I will not be long, I just want to serve these customers, then attend to you,' Fity assures JT. She believes that JT was impatient and, as a businesswoman, did not want to lose a customer. But JT's problem was somewhere else. He was not interested in plantain but Sergeant, who could help him leave the country. 'Man does not live on bread alone.' JT's priority now is not to eat and live but starve and leave. All the pennies must be saved to make the cost of travelling. He has some savings but did not know how much the trip was going to cost him.

'Madam, can we have some fried plantain for two hundred CBEE and two fish please,' JT makes an order for two as Sergeant appears with a large smile.

'Sure, it will cost you six hundred CBEE, sir.'

'No problem, we are in the corner there.'

'Okay.'

'So, what can I do for the "man of God",' Sergeant started with irony again, having received the news about the church conduct.'

'Please, I cannot deceive myself here. I am just like you, maybe now nobody, and want to seek your assistance. Please save my head, Sergeant.'

'I am listening. I will do my best.'

'Well, it is about my travel project. It is now urgent. Please do what you can so that I can leave this place as soon as possible.

'I thought you wanted to take your time and prepare the trip properly.'

'Yes, I said that, but circumstances have changed, and I cannot wait any longer.'

'What has changed? Why do you want to leave now? Have you won the lottery?'

'You are my brother, and I cannot hide anything from you. Look at this paper.'

Sergeant could not help himself.

'I do not think there is anything funny about this story. My name will come out here and I cannot live to see such a humiliation,' comments JT.

'I seriously sympathise with you. I did not mean it; it is your reaction that makes me laugh.'

'Put yourself in my shoes, I am anxious about people's reaction to this news. Will I not be seen as a bad guy, an adulterer? Who will defend my records? The common man will believe that I did all this out of wickedness.'

'I know you are a good man, and it is for that reason you have been used. The women in our church are also used by the prophet. But they do not know. Their testimonies help the prophet in his effort to get a larger congregation and make more money. What you do not know is that I, myself, was in that position before you joined the church.'

'Are you kidding me?'

'No, I am serious. I was the man to bring men to church or get the women pregnant, and then we say that God has performed a miracle in the lives of those women. They are victims, and it is difficult to explain that to them or any member of the congregation; no one will believe you and you become a villain. Who are you to go against the work of God, they would say, but which God are we talking about? Then we receive envelopes full of money. So, I know how miracles are performed in that place. I was about to leave when you joined. So, when the prophet turned to you, it was a relief for me. I did not know how to warn you in case you thought I was becoming jealous. So, myself, I am leaving for an Eastern European country next week. I got my visa two months earlier. I was just waiting for the end of the cold season. I am going to Minisor, a country near the Siberian Sea. Who knows, my name may come out as well, which I doubt.'

'What does that mean for me? Would you be able to help me before you travel?

'Which country do you have in mind?'

'USA.'

'I cannot help you with your USA plan. Why don't you go to Europe? Tetnov will suit you best. I am going to Minisor because I have a relative there. If you do not want too much trouble, go to Tetnov; they still need cheap labour. Entry levels are high for other countries, and they speedily send people back. You can try your luck, but honestly, I would not advise you on those destinations. It took me more than two years to raise the money I needed. I would not risk my hard-earned money on a route with a high probability of being sent back. I do not have any parents or relatives that can sponsor me. You people are lucky, your uncle can help you if you blow what you have now.'

'Please do not twist and turn the knife in my wound. I may have an uncle with megabucks, yet I live in scarcity. I'm only a domestic worker for my uncle. So please if you can help me, do it for the sake of God. Consider that I have no one to assist me financially. My mother is a widow in the village. She cannot even afford her transport to the capital, let alone overseas trips.'

'What do you have in mind? What would you like to do over there? I hope you will make a difference, many people I know who have the chance to reach Europe put aside their knowledge and dwell in menial jobs. There is nothing wrong with taking up a less glamorous occupation upon arrival. However, once you have settled, you must be looking into a more rewarding job. You must think about what could help your continent. Consider yourself as an investment that must yield a return for the continent, although no one sent you on this adventure. You must be ambitious. If you work hard, you will be rewarded. Over there, they do not care about the colour of your skin or who your parents are or where you come from. What they care about is your ability, skills, knowledge. Are you useful to society? That is what they are after. They are not divided into ethnic lines like what you see here. Here you get to a government office and behold, people are speaking their dialect. This does not happen in that part of the world. So, once you get there, you must change; do not ask those silly questions like where are you from? Do not call people by the name of their country of origin like our people do here. Learn good manners, respect the laws of the land. If you break the law, they will send you back here. Animals have rights there unlike in your country where, once you see an animal, the next thing you think of is food. If you kill birds or squirrels you see in cities, you will be in trouble. Do you understand?'

'I am with you.'

'You may think I am being funny, but those simple things may put you in trouble. They can deport you for violating those values: human rights, animal welfare. One more thing, once there, forget about polygamy; your people marry many women here and you treat them like second-class citizens. Domestic offence is a criminal offence, so be incredibly careful, respect women, brother. So, getting back to the main subject, if you know your subject well, you will get good employment, but do not be average. You need to be bloody good. Competition can be harsh, so be prepared to fight. You must go the extra mile to get what you want.'

'I will, trust me. I will not disappoint you if you help me cross over.'

'Do you have money?'

'Yes, I do. I have got some money, but I am not sure if it will be enough for the trip.'

'Good! Would you have at least 2.5M CBEE?'

'Yes, I think I may have it, the prophet paid me for that dirty job, and I saved the money for my project.'

'Good man, why don't we meet tomorrow at 1pm in front of the office of "One Man Plane" on Central Avenue.'

'That will be great,' JT replies with excitement. 'Now I can go home and sleep.'

The following day JT asked for a one-way ticket to Bezalazur, but he was told that the company does not sell one-way tickets for tourists, since they are supposed to return. 'So how much is a return ticket,' JT asks?

'It's in the region of 2.7M CBEE, sir,' the receptionist responds.

'What? That is expensive.'

'Sir, it is high season and late reservation. Advanced ticket will cost you 2.5M CBEE, a saving of two hundred thousand CBEE. Would you like to do that?'

'No, I don't want to take that chance.'

'You will also need a room reservation with the ticket to be able to enter the country. Further costs could be that of travel insurance. Your total cost will be around 3.5M CBEE.'

Sergeant suggested they withdraw to discuss their options as JT only has 3M CBEE at his disposal.

'Why don't you join my cousin in the country of the brave men? He works at the president's private residence near the border. You should not have any problem. This will allow you to raise the balance undisturbed. Once you have what you need, I'm sure you will not need my help.'

'Sure, I think it is a brilliant idea. I need to leave the country now.'

CHAPTER 8

JT has a great esteem for Maputa, the country of 'brave men' and its inhabitants. The people of Maputa never tolerate nepotism, and cronyism that is inherent to some poor countries. They not only raise their voice but act when the political class engages in malpractices. The leaders of the country that are historically the descendants of a large kingdom of Soulou really stand out. Their current leader, President Monory is the great-grandson of Fahama, considered as a powerful example of resistance to foreign invasion. He was a ruler and state builder who held colonial power at bay for two decades and created one of the most powerful, best-organised states in West Africa. JT listens to songs about Fahama's heroism in the fight against the invasion. To serve his great-grandson was a dream come true for him. He was given the role of servant at the president's residence near the border with Kombi. JT quickly grew in the job and attracted the attention of the guards. He always volunteers for things that are not his duty. His approach to running the residence and advice to the guards made him look more like a consultant than a mere servant. On one of his retreats, the president noticed the difference in how the house is being maintained. The president outside the office was a down-to-earth man. He communicates with staff at his residence with consideration and this shocked JT. He is one of the fans of the president, but he did not realise that the man was also good to those who served him.

The president was so impressed with JT that he promoted him to the rank of guard to have him close to him. JT was grateful once more to Sergeant for directing him.

President Monory has been a great leader and was praised by his people until his international backers cooked up a suicidal approach to economic reforms. He lost control over the economy as he was ordered to scrap all forms of subsidies to local farmers. Multinationals took over government-backed agencies and poor farmers became poorer. The people became disenchanted and began to question their leader's strategies and conduct. They wondered whether their president had turned his back on them. They began to raise their voice. Thus, halfway through the second term, he decided to revise all existing contracts with multinationals. Many of them lost their contracts, others saw some clauses removed from their contracts.

Following his third victory, President Monory organised a private party at his private residence hundreds of miles away from the capital. He invited some foreign diplomats and dignitaries from his village. He gave a speech that left some invitees confused over the message. But the people from the village grasped the message well. As the party draws to its conclusion, he slips through the back of the residence near the riverbank. He calls upon his ancestors and father who fought relentlessly against foreign invasion. He faces the monument he built on his father's tomb to ask for his blessings. JT was curious to see the president venture into the darkness alone. So, he decided to follow him at a reasonable distance. 'This man is really entrenched in our tradition.' But what followed shocked him; a gunshot was fired. He ran to the president who was covered in blood. He ran back to the house like a mad cow. 'Help! Help!' He was undeniably concerned that people would accuse him of assassinating the president. The partygoers dashed in his direction and confirmed the death of the president. But JT could not see where the fatal bullet came from. The international media reported that the newly elected president has been assassinated by his personal guard who followed him at a distance as the president requested the support of his ancestors for the new term in office. 'A twenty-six-year-old man is being questioned. He may not have acted alone. Mass arrests are planned to identify the mastermind,' a source close to the presidency stated. Some high ranked military personnel that were unsure whether JT had identified the killers or not decided to get rid of him. 'In the absence of witnesses, the case could be closed,' they were reasoning. So, they dropped him off at night at the border.

'If we see your face in this country again, it's your body that will be sent to your parents in a bag. Do you understand?' a soldier warns him.

'I will leave this continent altogether,' he appeals to them in a trembling voice.

'You better.'

They drove off and stopped at a reasonable distance. 'Lieutenant, we have made a serious mistake. We should finish this guy so that all possible witnesses are wiped out,' the driver, and second in command suggested.

'Go on, finish him,' the commander orders. 'You have ten seconds to say your last prayer,' the deputy commander advises JT. So, he moves away from him to a reasonable distance and fires at him a couple of times.

'Job done, Lieutenant. Let us go.'

'Get behind the wheel and keep it to yourself.'

'Trust me.'

The dead man woke up five minutes later; he was so frightened that in the middle of his prayer, he passed out before the soldier fired at him. He touched his body and realised that he was still alive. He stood up, looked back. There was no light, the pick-up had vanished. He ran for his life in the darkness. He followed the road ahead and shortly slipped into a light forest and ran parallel to the main road. He ran without questioning any common sense. He just wanted to go as far as possible from the country border and the soldiers. There came a time when he wanted to stop running, but the fear of danger that the forest presented made him continue. He worried that he could be attacked by animals. There could be dangerous snakes in the trees. Perhaps there might be a town or farm nearby. But there was no presence of human beings near the border. So, he joined the road and continued his run. After hours of running, he got exhausted and fell by the roadside. He was later picked up by an early coach to Gadu.

'So, these soldiers were going to kill me for witnessing President Monory's death. They are crazy. They know that I did not do anything wrong. Is it how people die?' He took a paper and wrote: 'Dear Mum, I am one of the luckiest people in the world. I could have been dead yesterday, but I do not know how God saved my life. Continue to pray to the God you serve. He did not want to put misery upon you. Your son is still alive. I escaped that midnight gunshot. The bullets missed me.'

But he reflected on how his mum was going to take it, since he did not have the intention to return to the village. Else, what interpretation the translator was going to give his mum without further details nor background of his short statement. So, he tore the paper. 'I must leave Gadu now. There are dangers everywhere here, whether it is at the central coach station or neighbouring countries. I must go where people do not kill for no reason.'

CHAPTER 9

Flight 202 landed at 6.45 am at terminal 1, San Baffo Airport in Tetnov on 29th June 1999. JT could not believe the time, 'It cannot be true, the sun is high in the sky for six am. This is the wrong time; it must be nine or ten am.' JT later realised that he was now in a different part of the world. He was shocked to find San Baffo Airport not too different from the airport in Gadu except that San Baffo Airport was busier and bigger. He could see normal human beings busy checking passports. JT got confused. 'Am I really in Tetnov? Uncle's friend, who works as a firefighter at the airport and has visited many countries, said that "A man who has never seen Bezalazur has not lived a worthy life." But what I am seeing does not instil confidence. These people look like me except they have a different skin colour, some even look smaller and shorter. They do not have big bellies. Do they really eat well? The airport is not that hugely sophisticated, would money be here, or did Sergeant send me into the wrong place? Well, you can't judge a book by its cover. I somehow trust Sergeant; he said this place was perfect for me.' JT was confident, but first he must go through the strong wall of immigration.

Tetnov is the land of dream and prosperity for many Africans, young and old alike. It has developed a reputation for imagination, delusion and expectation and a pole of attraction for the many discontented whose aspirations have been shattered by bad policies and cronyism. The land in Tetnov brings wonders and inspirations. It bears none of the deadly diseases that decimate populations across the world. Its hospitals are forced to refuse bookings year in, year out due to high overseas demand for health MOT. Politicians in Africa trust its facilities and physicians. The children in Kombi wear T-Shirts that promote celebrities in Tetnov. They know the names of Tetnovian soccer champions as well as their best players. Local Kombian football teams name their teams and players after major football clubs in Bezalazur. It is all green in Tetnov; no one is poor nor unable. Young women look like Miss World while young men behave like film stars. Surely, the land of Tetnov must be blessed and must be different from that of Gadu. The people fight for those they have never met and do not know. They support many good causes and help the poor. They fight for equality and human rights. They fight for women's rights too. They must live in mansions with many cars and maids and possibly plenty of money to spare. They enjoy themselves. They go on vacation to hotter places in the world and stay in expensive hotels. It is with this picture of Tetnov in mind that JT stepped on the 'One Man' aircraft in Gadu. JT dreams of an airport where all buildings are glass. He supposes that people will be lifted and dropped from point A to point B by a sort of machine at the airport. He also imagines immigration officers to be as big as baseball players. They must have a big belly behind a glass desk. The excitement and anxiety of discovering a new world kept the adventurer awake prior to and during the flight.

It was also the first time JT had got on an aeroplane and he was so anxious that it was hard for him to close his eyes in case anything went wrong. He prayed that God would save the lives of all passengers on the plane. He was amazed to hear some passengers snoring. 'Don't they know that our lives are at risk? They are sleeping as if they were in their own bedroom! These people don't care about life.' He had his Bible on his lap. 'Surely God will help in the event of a crash,' he strongly believes. He followed every single movement of the plane whether it was air turbulence or loss of altitude. He was daydreaming at the same time. 'Am I really leaving my native land? When will I see this land again? Will I see Mum alive on my return? What if Mum falls sick or dies while I am still there. Who is going to help Mum with farming? What is there ahead of me? Will they allow me in? I think so. Will I be able to achieve my dream? I believe my life will change over there for the better. Once I get a good job and have made money, I will be able to support Mum. I will also be able to build her a house. Those who mock Mum now will be sorry for themselves. Perhaps I will be able to help the whole village and lobby the regional government to do something for our area. I am sure Mum will look for a woman for me. She believes she could make the best choice for me. Doesn't she know that I am not just after beauty, but someone who will understand and trust me? I do not want someone who will push me into an unsustainable lifestyle. There are still a handful of good girls there, but the reality is that many young people aspire to travel to this part of the world. They can play the game to hook you in; no one knows who is genuine nowadays. But our God is faithful, and he always guides his children. Maybe I will ask Mum to find someone for me. But if I do so, would she not get me a village girl? I am quite sure she would. She has never been to the city.'

JT was out of breath when he saw the immigration desk as if he had been running for hours on end. Whether a visa is genuine or fake, facing an immigration officer is worse than appearing in a criminal court. In court, the accused are represented by lawyers. At the immigration desk, there are no lawyers or jury to assist the officers in their decision-making. For some migrants, a refusal of entry is comparable to a denial of access to wealth, freedom, hope and a better future. A degree gained in Europe gives the holder access to lucrative positions in Africa. To this end, those who can, prefer to complete their education in the Western part of the world. Thus, a refusal of entry has a lasting implication on a student who put his faith in earning a degree from a credible institution in Europe. For the economic migrants, denial of entry is an utter condemnation of poverty. These poor people are used by political cronies as potential human shields and demonstrators for political parties. They are the ones to become war casualties. This drum plays in the mind of any African approaching an immigration desk and by the same token, the immigration wall becomes a frontier between life and death for some.

'Sir, what is the nature of your visit?' an immigration officer asks JT.

'Study,' JT answers.

'Good! Can you confirm for us the address of the school and the nature of your course please?'

'First Pass, Dual Carriage Way, Southwest Two. I have enrolled on a six-month course for university entry. I plan to enrol at the school of human biology. I studied medicine in my country, but I could not complete the degree.'

'Why?'

'I became sick and spent more than two years in the village.' JT decided to keep a long story short.

'Who is your sponsor, sir?' asks the officer.

'Sponsor? Sir, I don't understand.'

'Who is supporting you financially?'

'Aha, no one, myself. Who do you think can support me financially?'

'Okay. How much do you have on you?'

'Herr, about five M CBEE.'

'What is that? How much is it in our currency?'

'It is about five hundred SK.'

The officer excuses himself to check some details with the school.

'Sorry about that,' he continues. 'How long are you staying?'

'Erm, six months.'

'What would be your address, sir?'

'I will spend the first two weeks in a hotel. After that, I will find cheaper accommodation.'

'Mr JT, you will suffer financially in this country with the cash you have on you. It could be enough if you had financial backing. However, as a student, you will be allowed to work part-time. Do you know anyone in this country?'

'No, I don't.'

'Surely you do not meet the entry requirements, but somehow, I feel like I should give you a chance. You are a lucky man. You can go. Follow the exit sign. There is a taxi stand on your left and a bus stop on the right, only the bus turns up every half an hour. Good luck with your studies.'

'Thank you, sir.'

JT could not believe how easy it was to beat the immigration officer at the Bezalazur airport. The relief to have made it through the immigration 'wall' was uplifting. JT was speechless when he heard, 'You can go, it is your lucky day.' The interview seemed smooth and straightforward. JT felt like someone whose lottery ticket had landed the jackpot. He was over the moon. He felt like speaking with his mum to tell her that he had crossed over but there was no facility to do so. 'So, it is simple to enter this country. I am going to become somebody. I will work hard. I promised to work hard, didn't I?'

Five minutes after JT had gone through the immigration desk, a man appeared at the bus stop. 'Are you JT?'

'Yes, I am. And you?'

'Attooo ("welcome" in an African language)! You made it! Praise God and welcome to the land of opportunities. Sergeant advised me to meet you at the airport in case, I am Zokoh. How was it?'

'Pretty simple, the officer asked me some questions about my studies and finances, that was all.'

'Don't mind them; here, you determine your future. If you

work hard, you will make it. Salaries here are good and we currently need staff at my workplace. My supervisor asked me yesterday to find two more people. You are lucky, you came at the right time. There is currently a huge demand for casual workers. Some people work during the day, I work at night.'

'You work nights?'

'Yes, I prefer night shifts; there is more money to be made working nights. You earn extra two SK. If you work hard here, you will earn more than a government minister in Kombi. Since I am still studying, it is convenient to work at night and attend lectures during the day. I save time by combining work with studies.'

'Excellent! What are you studying?' The look of Zokoh gives some confidence to JT. 'If this man is still studying, then I can. He does look older to me.'

'Is it not hard to work and study? What time have you got to rest?'

'I am in my final year of banking. You know, my friend, there is no time for rest over here. That time will come. But bear in mind that it takes character to make it here, no doubt. Are you ready to start work tomorrow?'

'Why not?'

'I am so excited to meet you, there are only a few people from Kombi in this country. We have an association that meets at the end of every month. I will let the president know now that we have a new member to our number of eleven men and women altogether. How is home?'

'Home is there. We will talk about home in detail later

depending on what you want to know.' JT was not really interested in talking about Kombi.

'Where is your stuff? The bus is due in two minutes.'

Before he could answer Zokoh, a man in uniform appeared behind him. 'Sir, follow me,' he orders. They walked back to the building and to the desk where JT just had his interview. 'Do you know the man who was talking to you well,' the officer asks.

'No, I don't.' JT's mind went back to his encounter with immigration officers at the airport in Kombi. 'Not prison talk again,' he thought.

'Be careful and smart in this country. Guard, lead him to the waiting room for the next departure.'

At first, JT believes he is being protected from strangers who could kidnap him. 'Is this country that dangerous? I thought the central coach station in Gadu was, but for the immigration officer to warn me of strangers is a sign of predators lurking in broad daylight. Should I tell them that the man who was talking to me is my countryman? Would that help or make things worse? What if they ask me about our conversation? This time the passport is genuine and so is the visa, so what is the problem?' What JT did not know is that he was monitored. The officer wanted to ensure that JT did not have any links in the country as he claimed. Some people enter the country on recommendation but pretend they know nobody in the country. It appears that JT knew someone who came to pick him up, this blunder is now taking him to a detention centre.

CHAPTER 10

Inside a poorly lit room on the ground floor of an iconic building at the airport, were waiting a dozen disoriented men. There is nothing significantly iconic about the building, dull with an unusual painting. The windows look small for the magnitude of the block that accommodates numerous offices. JT sat quietly on a wooden bench. He refuses to acknowledge the dark faces around him, with reddish eyes almost buried in their skulls. A total silence reigns in the room. No one knew exactly what was going on and it was awkward to ask a stranger. An hour became two, which became three and then four hours of agonising wait for the people who expect to hear their name when some officers enter the room. Those who are called out are escorted to an unknown direction. JT was hoping to hear his name, but that was not the case. After a while, the doors opened. 'Come with me gentlemen,' a guard commanded. All those who were waiting rose without a single world. The atmosphere was sombre. A coach was waiting outside the door. Two men in blue and black uniform stood on each side of the coach, eyes fixed on the passengers to ensure no one slipped away. All the travellers had to do was to step in from the staircases. They all boarded for an unknown destination.

Perhaps they were going to the capital, some were thinking. However, something was not right. Everything indicated that they were going to a kind of temporary place for the night or a kind of prison. After a short drive, the coach stations and a heavy gate opens to let all passengers in. They were shown where they were going to spend the night.

'Is the capital that far?' one of them broke the silence.

'No,' answers another one, who seems to know the place.

'So, when are we entering the city then? Why are we in a place that looks like a prison?' the man asks again.

'Entering the city? Which city? We are going back,' replies another one.

'What? JT asks in a trembling voice.

The man who seems to know what is going on begins to talk. 'We are lucky to be here. You realise that the security guard called some names out?'

'Uh-huh,' they respond in unison.

'Well, those ones were being deported immediately. If we are still here and hanging on, then I believe they could not find seats for us on return flights to Africa. Hopefully, we will make it to the main detention centre where we could be given more time to make our case. However, if they secure seats on return flights to Africa tomorrow, then bad luck. Conditions here are not adequate for the number we are. They detain people here for twenty-four hours and send them back. So, our prayer is that they do not call our names tomorrow. I came with a visitors' visa that turned out to be a fake one two years ago and I was returned after two days in this place. We cannot stay here for more than two days. So tomorrow they will call again whoever has got a place on a return flight.'

'That is crazy,' JT reacted angrily. 'I was cleared to leave the airport, only to be called back by a security guard after I had exchanged a few words with somebody I did not even know. The person claimed to have been sent by someone from my country.'

'Really?' the man mused. 'I see what happened, they believe you have already got a family here. Because certainly you told them that you did not know anyone here and someone suddenly appears, this amounts to a lie, I am afraid. They cannot trust you any more as a genuine person; you have lied once, that is it.'

'But I told them that I did not know the person who was sent nor the person that may have sent him. Why did they not confront the person who spoke to me to know the truth?'

'There was no need. You could both be lying.'

'I am not a liar. I am going to talk to them now.'

'You could try, but I doubt you will be able to do so. It is no point crying over spilt milk. The only avenue you are left with now is getting a lawyer to represent you.'

'The day I see this Zokoh, I will deal with him harshly. Who sent him anyway? I do not think it is Sergeant, he would have told me. I was already at the entrance door. Now chances are that I may be deported and die from humiliation and depression. I pray that God deals with Zokoh. I hope he will bear the consequences of his actions on his conscience forever.'

Then comes a long and agonising night, a night of living dangerously. 'Anything can happen now. Any name could be called now. There is no defence, no lawyer nor advice currently. Our hearts are beating fast. Our prayer is that other names are called tomorrow. It is insane, but that is human nature. You wish bad luck to others in those circumstances. I can now see the village, the farm and city at the same time. Would it not have been better to remain in Gadu and face humiliation? I have now wasted the little money I had to be near the promised land that now sounds far away,' JT was reflecting in the temporary detention cell. He nevertheless managed to steal three hours of sleep. He woke up to the reality of living in a cage. He must think about what to say or do when his name is called.

Two names were called the first day and three the second day. However, the number of people in the centre was not falling substantially as every day brings newcomers. 'So, while we are here, we must think about what to tell them so that they do not send us back. It is now the game of seeking compassion. They have denied us entry to the country like that. This means our visas are now invalid, whether student or visitors' visas. They believe that we applied for students' visas to gain entry, but we are not genuine students or do not have enough money to support ourselves, that is what they think. We cannot win over the student visa argument,' a man advises JT.

'Gentlemen, come with me,' a security guard orders again. This time it takes about two hours to reach a huge gate, a place that looks like a notorious prison centre. Electric bars, security guards at the four corners of the building and a type of airport search speaks volumes of the new centre. JT and three other men walked in line behind a security guard to room seventy-five in the last block of a 148-room establishment. They walked for five minutes going through long, stark corridors with cold polished floors. They walked past several metal grilles and cells furnished with little more than bunk beds. The men were welcomed by barely screened toilets and four plastic chairs, and four bunk beds. The room was rather small to accommodate four men. It was getting late for lunch when the four inmates received some instructions from the guard on the codes of conduct at Camp X.

'Welcome to Camp X,' the guard says. 'This is your room; the toilet is here right in front of you giving you the liberty to use it at all times. The shower room is in the grey building over there between block M and N. These are your lockers. Mr JT, you are number CX1752005. Here you go, this is your key. Inside you have a pair of tracksuits and flip-flops, they are all yours. Breakfast time is at seven forty-five, lunch at one pm and dinner at six pm. Bedtime is nine pm. No light, no noise after nine pm. Whoever is caught talking or outside his cell after this hour will take a cold shower at six am the following morning, and as punishment he will skip his breakfast, you got it?'

'Yes, sir,' they answer.

'Important note, you must remember your ID number. You will not be served food without this number. You must not leave this camp without permission. No visitor is allowed here except for your lawyer in the reception room.'

He shut the door and left. A deep silence fell upon the four inmates. The men look terrified. They suddenly felt wracked with anxiety and depression. There were no windows. There was no clock either to indicate the time of the day. Unless you wear a watch, you will never know the time of the day except you are called for breakfast or lunch. Thus, for the detainees, a day is split in three blocks: breakfast time, lunchtime time and diner time. In between, inmates sink into reflection and prayer for a day of freedom to come. JT felt the presence of people with lips sewn shut with anger, suffering and flashbacks. 'I hope this is one of these nightmares,' JT sighs.

Doors open for a call for dinner. On the menu: chicken and rice served on Styrofoam plates. Breakfast was served in the morning, but JT could not eat properly. He was concerned about the idea of being deported at any point of time. The reality was sinking in gradually, day one.

'Do you have a story?' an inmate asks JT.

'Which story?'

'A story that will save your life, ensure your stay in this country.'

'That is my worry, I don't have any story.'

'Well count yourself among those who are going home soon. You may be the next on their list.'

'Why don't you help me weave one quickly instead of wishing me bad luck?'

'Are you from the country where a coup d'état took place recently?'

'No, I am from Kombi.'

'But Kombi is currently in turmoil following last year's coup d'état as well is it not?'

'It is.'

'Then build your story around the turmoil in Kombi.'

'I understand. Can we not get a different story? I am not a politician. I was there as a guard to make a living. I will be uncomfortable answering any question related to politics. I am not interested in politics. Politicians are not trustworthy. They lie to voters. They corrupt people on their way up. If necessary, they kill even their best friends. I do not want to be affiliated with politicians.'

'You do not get it, it is not about being a politician, it is about how the politics in your country affects your life and especially how the current social unrest is a threat to your life. If you stay in your country, you can get killed. So, the point you want to make is that you are running for your life to a safe place. Does that make sense to you?'

'Yes, but will they not associate me with politicians?'

'No, they will see you as a victim. They know and understand more about politics than you do. This is a survival game. Do you want to lie once and survive or tell the truth once more and die? What would your future once back in Kombi?'

At this point, JT went quiet. He does not have any future in Kombi. JT did not want to be associated with politics because of the incident at President Monory's residence. He does not want anyone to know that he witnessed the president's death. 'Right, I got you,' JT replies. 'How do I construct this story?'

'Well, if you can prove that you cannot return to your country for fear of being killed then you can stay. If you claim asylum, then you will be granted legal representation to defend your case. Put it this way, are people close to the general not being targeted and killed? Are your people not being indiscriminately abused, imprisoned and silenced?'

'Yes, one of my schoolmates got killed. And what is your story?' JT asks.

'I was teaching political sciences and human rights at the national university of my country. I believe my views were reported to authorities. They saw me as a danger, someone who stirs troubled waters, someone who may cause revolution in the country. You know, in my country there is no freedom of speech, nor human rights or democracy. Winner takes it all; there is no opposition party. The next person who raises his small finger to grumble his discontent is jailed, no questions asked. If you are a businessman and your affairs are doing well, you become an enemy and threat to the power and you must also pay the price. If you voice your concerns over the state of governance, you become a prisoner. Defending democratic values or human rights lands you in jail if you are lucky. Elections are rigged and constitutions are changed overnight to suit the incumbent president. Our politicians do not defend any manifesto; they do not fight for any ideology, but to have access to national resources. They are not different from robbers except that they have forced their way to get a mandate to steal. It is unthinking that politicians are the wealthiest people in Africa, not businesspeople. It is irritating to see them loot the country and go unpunished. I believe African leaders are ignorant in general. I do not blame them because none of them studied politics. They came to power by force, through coup d'état and rebellions. It is really a shame. It makes Africans look like uncivilised people. They do not know really what the high office stands for. They abuse the trust of the electors. If a poor man turns into a millionaire overnight, what do you think he will do with the money? For him, all things are permitted. So, you are right to run away from politics if you are a God-fearing person. At the same time though, would you allow those crooks to plunder all the national resources and cripple the continent? What is your contribution if you do not stand against malpractice? Politicians take people for fools and the people take themselves for beggars and servants; they ignore their rights. They put one person in office to organise and share the resources of the nation, then that person becomes so powerful, so strong and mightier than the whole nation and subdues them, rendering them potential prisoners if they claim their rights. It is incredible, it is beyond comprehension, and it is madness altogether. My job was to raise those issues, which unfortunately put me in trouble. Perhaps it may have been better to bury one's head in the sand. What the eye cannot see is unlikely to cause heartburn. Anyway, so one day I got arrested for no reason. I spent over a year in a prison cell, but with the complicity of a prison guard I escaped. I left the country for Maputa but fell into the trap of civil war. So, I flew from Maputa to this country as a broke. The officer was concerned that I would become an eventual liability for this country. These are the key factors that play against you when you are financially unable. However, I applied for asylum. I am here with you, it's time to get a solicitor that can establish my case in a way that is acceptable to the authorities. Once I have a lawyer, I believe I will be out.'

JT's brain starts working. All night he could not sleep. As well as compiling his own story, he has compassion for the professor. 'Politics has destroyed this man's future, such an asset to Africa. How can Africa continually lose its bright children? This must be stopped. Men like this man are supposed to be travelling across the continent to give conferences on good governance. But he is here now and who knows, he may never return to Africa again; a 'lost son'. What are his options if the system here rejects his application? Where would he possibly go? When is Africa going to change?' he was reflecting. 'Do these politicians understand the meaning of life? What are they going to do with all the money they are embezzling? Why are they so selfish and so egocentric? I think all former African heads of states who looted while in office should finish in prison. This should serve as a deterrent to future leaders.'

Camp X operates long hours of cell-locking to teach wealth-seekers a lesson of no pain, no gain. Detainees are kept behind bars during the day at the guards' mercy, between breakfast and lunch or lunch and dinner. There are toilets in each room, therefore no need to move around. There was nothing to see or enjoy outside the four walls anyway. In that sense, would not being indoors better than outside? Camp X has different reasons for keeping its detainees indoors. The guards want to be the big and bad guys in their industry. Perhaps their notorious reputation will grant them more government contracts.

At Camp X, the food offered is repetitive and bland and served on Styrofoam plates for fear that spoons, and knives turn into fatal arms. Some detainees are told they are lucky to receive their rations every day. Detainees can wear their own clothes, but drab tracksuits and flip-flops are provided for those who need them. JT never complains about what goes into his stomach. He is rather concerned about the indefinite detention which some have compared to 'death row'. While some security guards show some compassion, many abuse detainees. Many are cruel and sometimes come up with ideas to humiliate and deprive them of their daily meals. Staff in the kitchen are equally divided on the treatment of the detainees. Those who have remained long in the centre chat to kitchen staff. Some kitchen staff in return call them 'residents'. But some staff serve foods as if they were obliged to do so. They particularly hate detainees who look proud as if they were 'important'. Those staff see asylum seekers as beggars who do not really deserve regular free meals.

While daytimes are times of fear, disdain and frustration, sorrow comes at night. Night is also a time of real isolation and a time when people succumb to their darkest fears. It is the time the guards remove people scheduled for deportation. The fear of waking up to the call by a guard keeps JT awake almost every night. Trauma and nightmares began to affect him. He became mentally feeble and distressed. His physical appearance altered with months in the centre. He began to neglect the basics of bodily hygiene. His thoughts became vague and negative. He sometimes stops thinking. Thinking is useless and makes the body weak.

Some days JT reflects on his living conditions. 'This place is a prison, look at the building! The wall is shielded with electric bars. Here, all your movements are controlled, you cannot go out, no one to visit you except for your lawyers. This is a prison except that you are happy to some extent to be inside, which means there is still hope that you remain in this country. We have rooms, but we don't need them. They are useless. We have beds, but there is nothing to do in bed. Beds are useless, we don't need them. We have a courtyard, but we don't need it. There is nothing in the courtyard; it is useless. We have inmates, but we don't need them. They are hopeless. Are they not lucky, those born in this land? They are free and cannot be detained, well, I mean they cannot experience what we endure behind these walls.' He was thinking about the natives he did not know that travel undisturbed. 'I am in a cage here while the wheel continues to turn. Why did the immigration officer put me here? Why me? Why do they select certain people, not everyone who crosses the border? What have I done wrong to be caged this way? Can they not understand that I am seeking a better life just as everyone does? Why should I be punished for aspiring to a better life? In my country, the government is bad, but it does not detain anyone seeking to enter the country. Would these people accept being put in such a place in a different country? This is not right. And with such traumatic scenes you see every day, how can one be at peace? Some families have been here for more than six months. Lord I pray that you spare me from a lengthy and agonising combat. No wonder why so many people here look like someone recovering from a long illness. I do not know the length of my sentence and how old I would be by the time they decide to free me. I am wasting precious time of my life, but they do not care or understand. I will never recover the time I am spending in frustration here. It is unfair. If they do not want me, let me go back and look after my mum.'

'Do you know that some women in the other building sometimes go to bed naked?' a man who had stayed over six months in the centre interrupts JT's reflection.

'Why?' JT asks.

'To avoid deportation,' the man replies.

'What?'

'Well, who can put a naked person on a plane, and especially a woman?'

'How can someone humiliate themselves to such a degree? This is a step too far.'

'That story tells you that no one here wants to go back. You see, people resist deportation not because they hate their own country, but because of people's attitude towards deportees. The stigma of being a deportee is what people fear the most. One who is expelled is like an outcast in some societies. The people back home are heartless. I do not know if it is wickedness or jealousy that drags them to such intolerable behaviour towards failed asylum seekers. I remember a deportee from Europe who received all sorts of names in the area where I live. In the beginning he fought anyone who called him names or mocked him. A time came when he had to give up the fight. He could not spend his life fighting everyone around him. It made him look like a mad person and people cross the road when they see him coming. His life was never the same again.'

JT was shocked, not only to hear about the awful story of women sleeping naked, but he was blown away by the man's command of the language, Zana is his name. JT normally avoids him. He has a weird attitude. In the middle of a conversation, he may just leave without excusing himself. He is withdrawn. He sometimes smiles at people for no reason. When asked anything, he looks down and walks away. This attitude annoys many in the camp. They believe he is an unsociable character. The only good thing about him, from the point of view of the inmates, is that he goes to the canteen late, at the time everyone is leaving the building.

'So, what is going on in this man's mind?' JT asks himself. 'Maybe next time Zana is in a good mood I will try and find out more about his life.' JT was making sense of what Zana had said. 'This could be me being deported. Satan get behind me. I'm not going back,' JT quickly overruled his own thoughts. 'Where would I stay if I were to be sent back? Uncle did not want to help me. His wife sees me as cheap labour, a man without ID or a future. So, she will make sure that I do not escape again. My presence is good for her; to drive the children to school, it is me. To check the homework, it is me, to do shopping, it is me. To wash the car, again it is me. But anything else, no one remembers me. Party time I look after the children. Holidays, I look after the house. And the church story will not go away either. I will have to eventually face the media and the husbands of the women I have impregnated. No DNA test will be carried for lack of facilities, but what if the children look like me? What would I do if the pastor asks me to take responsibility? Moral issue, is it not? Would I look into the children's eyes and deny them? Would the women be on my side? Lord have mercy!'

One night, JT was woken by a bright light in his eyes. He saw a huge statue standing right in front of his bed. 'Your number please,' the guard asks.

'CX195 ...' JT answered as his mind went blank.

'Wrong number, you know the rule. You must present at the shower at six am for your punishment. Do you understand?'

'Yes, sir,' he replies. 'What is this? What did he expect? Was I not sleeping? This guard is evil. God will punish him. I know what to do to avoid thirty minutes of cold-water next time.'

'You are not having breakfast today?' Professor Theya asks.

'No, I am not. Don't you remember the rule? I had a cold shower this morning.'

'Sorry, JT. Yes, cold showers mean no breakfast. Sorry, my friend.'

JT did not have any appetite anyway. He is more concerned about his immigration status. 'Man does not live on bread alone,' he thought.

CHAPTER 11

The number of inmates doubled in each room while the number of beds remain unchanged at Camp X. Queues to the canteen extends to the 'prison' gate. 'Yes, this is a prison. Is it there a correspondent name? No.' Long-term tenants raise alarms to prison authorities who ignore their demands. Surveillance devices and methods of intimidation increase to impede on basic human rights, limited access to public areas and fresh air. Some detainees were now wishing to be deported. The transitional centre has now become a permanent residence for some families. Human rights groups denounce inhuman treatment of asylum seekers across detention centres in the country. Many demonstrations took place to urge the government to improve the living conditions for refugees and asylum seekers in detention centres. Tension mounts among the inmates. Almost every day a new arrival increases the number of inmates to further degrade the living conditions. The system was on the brink of collapse while the backlog of cases piled up. Despite numerous protests by human rights campaigners, Camp X took no action to improve conditions. Deportations were carried out in horrific ways. There was one winner amidst the chaos: the human removal organisations.

So long as people are being removed and bonuses are being paid, it is business as usual. Many inmates, including JT, went on hunger strike to make a point, but this action brought no change. The government did not want to waste resources nor improve conditions to attract more refugees. A man tried to escape the camp but was electrocuted by the numerous electric bars that secure the building. 'We are in the soup,' staff at the camp exclaim. 'What do we do with the body? What can we tell his parents? Can they sue us for the loss of their son? How do we get rid of the body?' The government took the body to his embassy. A letter sent to the embassy read:

'Your excellency,

It is with our deepest regret that we return the body of one of your citizens who passed while awaiting the outcome of his claim for asylum in this country. We endeavour to determine the exact cause of his death. We will update you as soon as the cause of his death has been established. Included is our contribution towards the cost of transportation and burial.

'Yours,

'The Ministry of Immigration.'

JT gave up the hunger strike at seeing the death of a detainee. 'There may be another way.'

Failed asylum removal is the time detainees' human rights are abused. It is the time the guards fully exercise their power over the detainees. All practices are good for an optimal result. A forced removal story has never been a tale of romance. Guards prepare themselves mentally and physically for any operation. They cannot fail. Their faces and eyes resemble those of warriors. Their body-build alone intimidates failed asylum seekers.

On one occasion, JT woke up to something unusual, a fight between a detainee and two security guards. 'What the hell are you doing? Get off the bed! You are causing delay,' they yell. 'If you want to see your parents again, get off the bed before I use excessive force on you,' one of them said. He continued: 'Look at me well, I don't joke with people like "you", pointing at him. JT opened one eye to have a glance of the interaction. The entire room was awakened, but no one really had the guts to say a word or stop the removal. Were the guards not performing their duty, even if the manner was disturbing? I do not want to get myself in trouble, JT covers his head. 'Right, enough is enough,' they said, moving things up a gear. 'We cannot miss our flight.' They finally overpowered the young man after almost half an hour of fighting. The twenty-five-year-old man has been clinging on to a bed frame to avoid deportation. They threw him inside an unmarked dark blue van and dashed away. They beat a couple of traffic lights and avoided a fatal collision at the entrance of the airport. They only had fifteen minutes on the clock by the time they reached the departure gate. They were exhausted but relieved to have made it. The fight continues at the airport. The man refused to give in and garnered sympathy from some travellers. Two hours later, he was back in the detention centre with a sense of victory. 'So, what happened?' fellow detainees ask in bewilderment.

'Well, God was with me today, some passengers fought my fight. A businessman on the plane and an elderly woman were appalled by the way the guards treated me. They refused to travel on a plane where a human being is strapped to a seat like an animal. The lady asked the security officers if they had children. "How would you feel if someone treated your child like that," she asked. "What is his crime? Even though he is undesirable in this country, could you not treat him with some dignity? How would his mother feel if she saw her son attached to a chair like a dog?" The businessman on the other hand threatened to not only get off the plane, but to sue the airline. The flight captain did not want any trouble. He advised the security guards to consider abandoning their plans. "Look, I do not want any lawsuit," he added. At this point, the officers gave in, but the return trip was a nightmare. I was called names, kicked on the head, slapped. They were upset that I had made the company lose money to the airline.' Apparently, the businessman had a bad memory of forced removal. He said that two years ago he experienced an incident on a flight that changed his view on deportation. He was travelling in business class when two security guards entered the plane with a young athletic looking man. He understood that the man was being forced to go back to his country. He said to himself, "Why can't these young and strong people stay in their own country and find something to do? It is good that he is being deported. This will deter others." The man was handcuffed, and his leg attached to his seat. At some stage he started complaining, his head down towards the knees in a corner with the guards on both sides. However, after a time he became quiet. The businessman said to himself: "Thank God, I am going to have some peace and quiet." What he did not know was that the young man was dead. A big scandal and panic followed on the plane. Sometime later, he was reflecting on how lucky he was to be alive. "Is life so fragile like this? Has this young man gone forever just like that? What for? Why should he lose his life like this? Perhaps I should have said something about his treatment rather than being content. He could have still been alive had he not been restrained in such an inhuman manner. My dad left a big business that I am running, which allows me to travel all over the world. Unfortunately, these people do not have that chance. I believe this is what that young man wanted to do, he wanted to leave a legacy for his children so that they would not go through what he had to endure. But that dream has now been squashed." He was so disturbed that he vowed to combat such practices. "It is my ambition to create employment in the poorest countries to offer job opportunities to desperate young people and reduce the level of economic migration. May God forgive those security guards who contributed to the premature death of such a man, so full of life."

The two men seriously abused me all the way back, insults upon insults, kicking my head. They were upset that I made them lose their bonus of the week. They said that they were also missing their target for the month. They promise to deal harshly with me next time. I have been warned. Do you guys know that deportation is a big business in this country?' the man continues.

'In what way?' they ask the man.

'The removal of failed asylum-seekers and people

overstaying their visas falls now into the hands of private companies, I learnt through the security guards' conversation. They are treated like VIPs when they land in Africa. They spend nights in five-star hotels. Not only are they paid for the work they do, but they also receive extra cash for leisure and entertainment. They were dreaming about a weekend in the sun in Africa today, but I shattered that dream. There are usually at least twice as many security guards as deportees. So, think about how much money is being poured into their pockets annually, millions of dollars, I guess. They were anticipating their boss's anger. He would not comprehend how two trained security officers could fail to restrain one man.'

'Are you saying that the government shelters us, feeds us, and pays staff in this place for some other businesses to benefit?' JT doubts. 'That is crazy! Why can't the government then pass on all responsibilities arising from the running of these centres to the removal of detainees? Payment should only be possible upon successful removal.'

'Mind you, I do not know about this centre, but I heard that there are other centres across the country run by private security firms.'

'That would make sense; even so, what does the government get in return? It seems to me that they get nothing in return except the creation of employment in that sense. The money wasted in detention centres could be well spent elsewhere. Are we not a commodity in this case? What are we producing? Nothing! We are liabilities here. The irony is that, after all, some asylum seekers will be allowed to stay while some are removed.

What is the sense of maintaining people in this centre, if they are to be released later?'

'Well, people would dodge the system and disappear if they were not kept in this place.'

'I do not buy the argument. They could let us do what we came to do while they investigate our case. At the airport I was asked to provide an address, which means that they will know where I stay. How can I vanish? The government could avoid spending money on us if they proceed by monitoring us while we study. This would instil confidence between us and the system. Imagine someone who has a suspended sentence; would he not be careful? We would be more careful and avoid breaking the conditions of our freedom if you want. But the present format is a resource drainer. I honestly believe the government is wasting taxpayers' money on these centres.'

'You make a valid point, perhaps the government gets something in return, who knows? Why don't you advise them?'

'I could if I were free, but look at us, we are prisoners, which means we have no rights at all. Our right to move, to speak and even sleep or get up when we want, has been confiscated. We are ordered to do things. We do not have a say.'

It was a victory for a detainee to escape deportation; many inmates were impressed with him. However, he was not usually so popular with his fellow inmates. They were fearful as, depending on the day, he could turn violent. He was also often very rude. JT heard that he had a fight with one of the security guards and a member of the kitchen staff. Others dismissed him as someone who is mentally sick. No one really relates to him. But when he gave an accurate account of his failed deportation, people were confused that he could express himself that way. Perhaps the possibility of being free one day positively activated his brain, and his current behaviour was a product of his treatment to date, the detainees concluded.

That night, JT found himself tossing and turning. He was traumatised by the story of forced deportation. He was now reflecting on his fate when a deep sleep came over him. In his dream, a guard freed him. JT put his black and white shirt on and headed to town. He met a couple of friends from university. Joy appeared on his face. 'You are missing breakfast!' a voice was heard. JT jumped out of his bed and realised that he was still in the detention centre. He is still in the hands of the immigration officers. His solicitor was now in possession of the transcript of his interview, but no decision has been made yet. JT was so disappointed that he refused to go for breakfast. He wished it were not a dream.

Friday afternoons seem to be the perfect visiting time by the immigration officers. As usual, they patrolled all rooms to ensure that all detainees are catered for. To JT's surprise, they looked at him for a second and went straight to their book. 'What is your name?' they asked. As JT confirmed his full name and date of birth, they said: 'You are going home next week.' Without further comment, they continued their touring.

'What? Am I really going back?' JT dashed to the toilet to ease himself. There is no one to run to, the man who used to advise him left the camp two weeks ago. Those who are in the camp are mainly people who are also likely to be deported, and fear and anxiety could be read all over their faces. They all look shaky and dominated by fear. Their minds are not straight enough to give any sensible advice to someone in distress. JT took the phone in a phone booth to call his solicitor who is nowhere to be found. 'What can I possibly do to escape? I cannot really, this place is secure enough. The lawyer has also abandoned me, he is not taking my calls. Does it mean that he cannot represent me anymore? The other man was lucky enough that people on the plane fought for him, will that be my case? What would I do if no one was willing to defend my case? My God is great and "what is written is written". Perhaps God wants me to see Mum alive. I am sure Mum would be happy to see me. I will not tell her my story; it may be painful for her. In addition, she may not make any sense of the story. She does not know about country boundaries. What do you call immigration officers in my language? The word does not exist. So, it will be difficult to give her a full account of this dramatic event. This seems to be the end of the road and the end of my life. I may just go to a neighbouring country and labour if that is possible. I do not think I will cope with life in Gadu or the village again.'

JT thought maybe Zana could appease his spirit since Professor Theya has left the camp. He was lucky to meet Zana in the right mindset. 'What is troubling you, my friend? You look frightened.'

'Well, I have received a letter from the Office of Immigration about deportation. They said I have only seven days left in this country.'

'Is there anything too hard for a man? To all problems, there is a solution. You are not the only one in possession of a deportation letter. It is what they said, but it has not happened yet. If you are not strong in your mind, how are you going to face the guards on the day? You can appeal the decision, or something can happen. Be strong as a man. A man is measured by the magnitude of his mind. Build yourself. Life experiences are the ingredients of valiant men, the role models you see in this world. You have just stepped into the shoes of men with history. Hold your cross with both hands. Listen, you may be aware of the tragic death of President Monory.'

'Yes, I am.'

'I was one of his ministers, minister for development. But with the mess around his death, everyone became suspect. I somehow knew that he was going to do something silly or be eliminated. He did not support the economic models imposed by his backers. He also opposed aid that fuelled corruption. Aid money gave unfair advantage to the ruling party. The money was used to corrupt some officials. He wanted to be judged on results. But with money being distributed by some of his ministers to voters, there was no way the opposition could compete. Consequently no one was really working for the development of the country. There were only two other ministers that like me supported his views on corruption. Now that he is no more, the new government decided to arrest myself and the other two on a corruption charge, ironically. Our assets have been frozen. What kind of life can I live over there? The three of us decided to leave the country so that they can loot the country unchecked. Sometimes I feel like hitting the wall. When I see myself eating on a plastic plate with a plastic spoon, I feel like taking my own life. I should not be in a place like this, and sometimes some of the kitchen staff would say "You are lucky to have something to eat three times a day. You look at food as if it's something disgusting. Would you have this in your country?" If only they knew that I had maids, chauffeurs, security guards ... So, what sort of conversation can I hold with those little boys around me here? Nevertheless, you must bear in mind that good things always come to those who wait. They may decide to deport you, but you must remain hopeful; anything can happen.'

A week later, JT woke up to a bright light again. 'Oh, you are not going to get me this time. I know my ID.'

'You, can you confirm your ID for us please?'

'Yes, it is CX1752005.'

'Correct, this is the number we are after. Follow us please.'

JT and three other detainees were scheduled for deportation. The heavy dark gate slams behind JT. He suddenly realises that they are being deported. 'Bloody hell, why did I confirm my ID to them? I should have given them a wrong number. Now I am trapped in their nest. I cannot escape. Soon, I will be in the air and back in Gadu. It will be pointless to ask about our destination.' It had been almost two hours, and JT was now convinced that they were going to the airport. Three other prisoners were in front of JT who sat at the back of the unmarked van. His heartbeat has changed suddenly. Total silence, each prisoner living a film of an unfulfilled dream. Their minds were on how they would be welcomed back by their respective families. JT knows that his cousins will be happy to see him back. Uncle would say, 'You should have been a little bit patient; I was talking to my friend in New York for you. You have now wasted this opportunity. Do you think it is easy to enter the European countries? Don't you know that our parents are poor, and we cannot take the risk of going abroad as other communities that have some support do?' This is the side that will hit him hard. 'Can we not break the cycle of poverty? No one is born poor nor rich, circumstances make the difference,' he was thinking. 'That is why I wanted to be in Europe to work hard and help Mum and my other brothers and sisters. Now the dark door has also slammed before me.' The van stops and one by one they exit the vehicle in absolute silence.

The two guards tried to be nice to them so that they did not have to fight. 'Gentlemen, you are going back, but after six months, you can apply for a visa again. Make sure that you prepare your case perfectly so that the government does not reject your application again. Get some evidence to support your statements. Do you understand? There are boxes that you must tick, you do not just come like that. So, remember the questions they asked you when you first entered the country and prepare the answers, it is as simple as that. We have success cases of people who were deported that have come back.' (They were lying.) JT only nodded his head. 'Okay now let's go, your flight is due soon.' This was the last flight of the day for West Africa. As they approached the tarmac, the story of the failed asylum seeker reported by a detainee came into to JT's mind. This also resonates with his own experience in the village after he had decided to return following the loss of his ID. 'How much would it take to call me Bengis while I never stepped outside the prison? I must not go, although I do not have any way to escape,' he was thinking.

JT looks into the guards' eyes and in an innocent voice says: 'I am not going.'

'You are what?' they ask.

'I AM NOT GOING,' JT replies in a loud voice that surprises the two security guards. They were not prepared for a fight. JT has presented himself as an innocent boy who had accepted his fate. They thought that for the first time they had an easy assignment. However, the job has taken a sudden turn for them to do what they were trained for; the use of force on those who resist. They try to twist the boy's arms at his back but fail to do so. They kick him in anger, 'You are wasting our bloody time, you ...' JT decided to defend himself and possibly delay the flight. 'If you kick me again, I will retaliate,' he says.

'You will what?' they scoff.

'I will slap you,' he replies to irritate them.

They punched him from left and right. The more they kick JT, the stronger he gets. JT did not know where his strength was coming from, but he managed to delay the flight by half an hour. He sustained a head injury and gave in. He was dragged to the plane 'half dead' but the flight captain advised them to take him to the nearest hospital. 'I do not want to bear any responsibility. I do not know what will happen to him in the next seven hours. So please call an ambulance or take him to the hospital now. I am not happy with what I am seeing. We are a country of law and order, and a safe country. We have all medical facilities, but I don't believe it is the case in Kombi. Further, we need to protect our reputation internationally.'

JT was taken to the nearest hospital.

'What happened to you, a car crash?' a patient on the next bed asks him.

'No, a fight with some security guards at the airport.'

'Which airport?'

'I have no idea, but it takes about two hours to drive from the camp.'

'Oh, you do not mean Camp X! That camp has a bad reputation.'

'That is where I am.'

'How do you guys live inside such a camp?'

'The thing is that we do not have any choice, and we do not know about other camps. We cannot protest, we take orders and pray to God that one day, we will be out and see life. We eat what is offered. We do not complain. But what we fear the most is the visit from the immigration authorities. Their visit has never been good news for us. They can look at someone's face and decide to send them back. So, as soon as one hears that immigration officers are around, Christians kneel and make a sign of the cross, while Muslims kiss the soil. How do you know about the camp, have you been there yourself? How far is it from where we are?'

'No, I have never been there myself, but we heard about it in the news. There are also reports that Amnesty International is fighting for more humane treatment for the detainees.

Here, we are on the outskirts of the capital,' the man continues. 'If you go out and look to the left, you will clearly see some tall buildings dominating the sky in the city centre. You are here, I mean the camp is here and we are here,' he says, pointing on the city map. 'The nearest town to your camp is this one here, and the capital is here. The camp is about thirty minutes away from the nearest town by car, and maybe an hour to the capital city.'

A week later, JT returns to the detention centre. The heavy metal door of the prison reopens and closes again. He is once again between four dark walls, after a time he counts as precious with a stranger who had given him an idea of his whereabouts in the country. Knowing his current location may be vital for an eventual plan for escape, although it will be foolish to attempt. No one can really escape. JT spent three further agonising months in the centre. The guards visit him regularly between 4 am and 5 am. The more visits JT receives from the guard the more he gives wrong answers. Sometimes he believes he is going to be deported and therefore he deliberately mixes the numbers. Occasionally he fails to give the correct answer due to panic. So, JT was missing his breakfast regularly.

JT's lawyer had reappeared and complained about his client being beaten and injured at the airport during a failed attempt at deportation. His client had sustained some injuries and needed hospital treatment. He kept the correspondence short to avoid animosity between him and the Ministry of Home Affairs. JT was not actually interested in compensation but permission to remain.

Six months after JT's escape from a failed deportation, good news came his way. Some representatives of the Universal Refugee Welcome Group (URWeG) arrived in the centre. A guard called on JT. 'You have a visit,' he said in a neutral voice. Yet JT's heart began to race. He recalled the visit by the immigration officers. He quietly followed the guard to the reception area. 'We are from URWeG. We received a letter from your solicitor that advised us that you are temporarily free. Following the incident at the airport, your solicitor launched an appeal to the Ministry of Interior, which has granted your temporary release. We are in the process of getting you a temporary accommodation. This may take a couple of weeks. One of us will come to pick you up once we have a place available. Expect our call soon.'

JT was over the moon. He spent all night dreaming about his days of freedom. It took two nerve-filled weeks before URWeG sent a confirmation letter that they have now secured a room for JT. However, the following morning, JT received another letter, this time from the Ministry of Interior, which read:

'Dear Mr JT,

It is with regret that we write to inform you that the Department of Home Affairs rejects your demand for political asylum in this country. The department received yesterday a communique from the embassy to inform us that the government in Kombi wants all refugees and asylum seekers to return. The government has set up a special committee to welcome all persons that left the country following the coup d'état. "We want to show the international community that we are a country of peace and prosperity. We do not want our citizens to suffer abroad because of our actions. We have all set aside funds to support them." This department concludes that, because efforts have been made in your country in human rights and peace and tranquillity have been restored, there are no grounds for you to seek political asylum in this country. International flights have fully resumed and diplomats, including those of this country. You have seven days to leave this country.

Yours sincerely,

The Ministry of Interior.'

'What is going on? What are these people playing at; one minute, you are free, the following you are detained? They are playing with someone's life.' JT rubbed his eyes and read the letter again, hoping that this time the wording would be different. Unfortunately, the wording remained unchanged. He picked up the phone and called his solicitor.

'Unfortunately, this is the current situation. We do not know what to do right now. This is an unusual case. We need to get grounds for an appeal, and this may take time. By the time we make an appeal, you may be in Kombi.'

'Are you saying that you cannot defend me anymore? I rely on you, and you are saying you will launch an appeal at the time I am already being deported, that is crazy!' JT dropped the phone. 'There must be a way. I am not going to take this lightly. I must fight for myself if the solicitor fails to act.'

CHAPTER 12

While some of those on the waiting list for deportation were on hunger strike, one of them thought about an irrational solution that would free all inmates. 'If this place were on fire, everyone would perish, including the guards that ill-treat us, right? Let me burn down this place and see what happens,' he plans. JT thought that the idea was not that bad, provided it is executed in a way to minimise losses. They set the centre ablaze, and the guards were left with no option but to open the gate and save lives including their own. Detainees were on the run. JT escaped without really knowing where he was heading to. He did not have a clue where to go; he did not know anyone in the capital. However, he has an idea of where the nearest city is, as well as a direction to the capital. But the capital is far away, and he would not take the risk of running there. He would go to the nearest town first and then find his way to the capital. He followed a couple ahead of him that seemed to know where they were going. After thirty minutes of stopping and starting, the couple gave up the run and returned to the camp. JT knows that the next encounter with the security guards would have a different outcome. They warned that he must be prepared for the next deportation project. Therefore, returning to the centre may not be in his interest. This fire break could be a blessing. He wants to take his chance, 'no risk, no rewards' – or rather 'high risk, high return'. He remembered that he must 'go the extra mile', according to the advice of his church brother prior to his leaving the country. Behold, a straight road appears before him showing the direction to the nearest town. 'Alleluia,' says JT in the hope that he might be free.

Three hours later, JT is in an unknown town with no money nor clothes for change or toiletry. He wanders around reading road signs, town centre maps and anything that can tell him about his location and the direction to the capital. He tries not to give away any signs that he is a stranger in the town. However, with no money, there was little prospect for him to reach his destination. He must eat, drink, and find a place where he can lay his head. The pressure was mounting at the thought that police could be after him. He needs to raise some money for food and transport to the capital. He tries to explain his needs to passers-by, but no one is interested in his stories. 'Why don't you go and get a job, you, lazy people?' one man says, pointing a finger at him. 'This is the man who posed as a homeless person last week,' another passing by says. 'I gave him 2SK and he is coming toward me again. I'm not a bank, why can't you remember those who have already helped you at least? I remember him,' the man adds and walks past. JT looked at him in amazement. But it means that there is someone who looks like him in town. He could survive then. He is going to pose as a homeless person. 'Help me please, I don't know where to sleep tonight and I have no money for food.' People walk past without looking, turning away as they reach his level. He has been standing for two hours. He sat down with his head bowed, and then coins started dropping next to him. He collected them and put them in a sock. A man in uniform stood near him for about five minutes to observe the traffic. JT kept his head in his hands. He could not move for fear of being identified as one of the escapees from Camp X. JT was sweating and breathing heavily. It was a road warden on duty, but JT did not know the difference. He only knows security guards and immigration officers. The five minutes last forever for JT, who nearly wet himself. Two hours later his pockets were full, but he did not know how much he had collected. He was not familiar with the currency but believes he has enough for a trip to the capital.

'How do I get to the capital?' he asks the restaurant manager.

'Over there is a bus to the capital. You need a correct fare; they don't give change.' JT jumped on the bus and took a seat at the back.

'Please let me know when we are close to Zone Blue.'

'I am afraid we don't go past Zone Blue,' the driver replies. 'You will need to change for another bus from station one.'

'No problem, thanks.' An hour later, the driver calls for 'station one' passengers. But JT did not realise it was his stop as he was not familiar with the bus route or the call.

'Excuse me, sir, are you not going to Zone Blue?'

'I am.'

'This is your stop,' a woman directs him. 'You need to cross over for a bus in direction to Zone Blue. Both numbers 7 and 49 go to Zone Blue. Read in front.'

'Thank you.'

After reconciling the list of detainees relocated to other detention centres in the country, one person was missing. The police decided to launch a fugitive hunt in surrounding areas. Unsuccessful, they extended their search to the nearest towns. Half an hour later, two police officers appear at the place where JT was begging. 'Have you seen this man,' the officers show JT's picture to people in the town centre.

'Yes, over there near the restaurant,' a woman directs. 'He is begging.'

'Many thanks.'

They rush to the point. 'He was here earlier but has now left for the capital. He may be still at the coach station,' the restaurant manager says. They moved to the station but were told that a man matching the description took the last seat on bus B1 to the capital about an hour ago. 'He must be in the capital by now,' a station attendant guesses.

JT has so far managed to hide every time he hears a police siren. His mind was not on food nor drink. He wanted to reach Zone Blue and try his luck with meeting the patient who gave him the map of the city again. Provided he dodges the police, he believes he will meet someone somewhere who will help him; he was convinced. He was also hopeful he would meet some West Africans in the market. The man he met in the hospital told him that there were some African shops in the market.

The people in the capital were different from those of the first town. Here people volunteer to help. They offer to guide him: 'Are you alright? Do you need help? What are you after?' they ask. JT was encouraged by the attitude of the people in the capital and was on course for a promised land. Unfortunately, he did not have any further reference; he is in Zone Blue but does not know what could be next except for locating the African shops. The people he bumps into give a vague direction to where African shops could be found. JT soon realises that Zone Blue is like a city within the city. Large avenues open before him. Long rows of shops and offices line both sides of a street that looks like a boulevard. He is tempted to walk along the street, but the street is busy with police cars. His instinct warns him to leave the main road.

He heads to a smaller street crossing a bridge to a place that looks like a marketplace. He made some enquiries, and someone directed him to an opposite street stretching over two hundred metres of width and ten kilometres long. The Africa market is located halfway down the street. He must find a place where he can spend the night in the capital. The good news is that at least, this time, he has some money on him, although he does not know the amount. He would not go hungry either, but he must now find a place to avoid sleeping rough again.

He heads towards an offside street that looks exceptionally colourful and vibrant. The street was remarkably busy with merchants bargaining perishable goods. They were shouting, 'All must go,' or 'Half price,' or 'Bags on offer.' JT was tempted to make a purchase, but before he checked his pocket, a car with a blue light was flashing and speeding towards him. JT vanishes into the opposite shop wandering like a businessman who wants to grab an item before he returns to his desk. He looked back and could not see the car anymore. He drops the idea of shopping and continues his road. Behold, two people in uniform were talking to some people a couple of metres ahead of him. He steps back and crosses the road again to avoid them. Two hundred metres later, a police car appeared behind him, and a sweating JT covered his face and turned his back to the street. The officers seem to be after a stolen car. Suddenly, Zone Blue appears to JT as a jungle. There was a possibility that he could be caught and returned to the camp. He could not see any way forward. He wished he could somehow become invisible. The people in uniform were now everywhere and he did not know which ones were after him. He began to cross the road dangerously.

JT reached a junction, but by this time he was getting exhausted. 'I must keep walking, what I'm seeing over there resembles the place the man described to me in the hospital. It looks like where the African market is. It may not be too far. God is great. I never lose.' JT looks left and right to cross the road, beholds two police officers pointing in his direction. JT assumed they were pointing at him. 'It may be him over there. That shirt can only be worn by a foreigner; it has to be him.' JT suddenly feels hot and begins to sweat. They were far away from him, but he felt their presence in his vicinity; he felt like their hands could grab him at any moment. He hears voices telling him to run before it is too late. 'I must run and vanish in the market. I stand more chance in the market than on my own on the street here. What would I say if they stop me?' He decided to beat the traffic. 'Bloody hell! Flipping heck, can't you check the traffic?' A heavy rattling and noise of breaking were heard. JT surely beat the first line of incoming cars but found himself on the bonnet of a white delivery van. 'Are you okay?' the driver asks an unresponsive JT. 'Oh my God, I am dead, I have killed somebody, but it was not my fault. He saw cars coming and ran into the road,' the driver consoles himself. Paramedics were called in and JT was taken to the nearest hospital with serious injuries. Miracle really! The driver of the van was shaken. He now worries about his driving licence and job. Worse, police were the main witnesses.

CHAPTER 13

JT's inability to talk poses an obstacle in the police's effort to locate the missing detainee from Camp X. Although the man in the coma matches the description they received on radio communication, it is impossible to confirm his identity and end the search. With no ID on him and unable to speak, the police officers remain in the dark about the could-be Camp X runaway and resolve to continue their search in the city while the suspect recovers from his injuries. They instruct the medical staff to keep an eye on the man.

A bright smile welcomed JT back to life after seventy-two hours in a coma. In clinical terms, the nurses believe the worst has been avoided. 'I am Dr Azemiah,' a physician introduces himself with a soft smile. 'You are making tremendous progress,' he adds. 'Soon, you will be reunited with your family. Nurse! take good care of him,' he says and moves to the next bed. Confusion added to JT's uneasiness as he found himself in a rather unfamiliar environment. His eyes blinked at the light as he tried to work out things by himself. The physician's words did not sink in as he could not comprehend what may have happened.

'You are in hospital,' the nurse said. 'You were involved in a serious road accident. You have been here for the past three days now. Thank God paramedics rushed you here in time. We believe the worst is over. Can we contact your family? Can we have a phone number?' There was no answer. 'Well, maybe he has not recovered properly yet. The good news is he can eat, which is a good sign,' the nurse thought. Another day passed and there was still no contact with the next of kin. The nurse was excited to give good news to the family but did not have any contact details. Failing to contact the next of kin, she must now get the patient's details. 'Can we have your details please?' she asks with a smile. So far, he is known as Mr 'T20' with reference to where the accident occurred.

'JT is my name.'

'Such a lovely and unusual name, where are you originally from?' she asks

'Kombi in Africa.'

'Oh, what a coincidence, my best friend is from Kombi, a lovely place I heard. I hope to visit Africa one day. Who knows, Kombi may be on the cards. So where is the family, can you remember now?'

'I do not know,' he answers.

'Not to worry, once your memory comes back, we will contact them.'

She moved to the next patient to check their temperature. However, before she leaves for another ward, two police officers appear for a witness statement. 'The officers are here to get a witness statement,' she says pointing to two men in grey and yellow uniform. 'Uniform again? They got me this time.

What can I say so that they do not take me now?' JT thought quickly and decided not to talk. They thought that he may have sustained a brain injury. 'It would be helpful if you could contact a psychologist,' they suggested to the nurse. 'We will give him some time, please contact us when he gets better.'

'We will,' replies the nurse.

Thus, a psychologist was called in to assess JT's mental status. The psychologist, Dr Dami, could not get much out of JT, who decided to be cautious. He wanted to ensure that the psychologist will not pass the information to the authorities. JT believes people may have doubts about his status in the country. If he could communicate with the nurse and the psychologist, but not the police, then there may be a problem with the authorities. So, at night, he worked out his plans to escape from the hospital. 'I know what to do, I will get the details of the nurse's friend, so that when I escape, I know where to go, brilliant idea,' he thought. JT was impatient to see the nurse in the morning, but she was not on duty. Instead, the police turned up again for an update. As they stepped into the ward, JT jumped out of his bed only to be grabbed at the gate by a security guard. The police tried their luck again unsuccessfully. 'We will come back,' they announced. 'Hopefully, he will be able to give us some clues next time.'

The nurse resumes work the following day. 'In a few days, you could be discharged,' she says. 'That is why we need to inform your family. They may be anxious and worried sick about your whereabouts. If you cannot remember any telephone numbers, which is normal in your case, we can pass your details to the police so that they can track your family,' she says, guessing that JT has lost his memory. 'They will be able to locate your family once they have their names. They are good at locating people, is it not part of their job? With them, you cannot hide.' JT was filled with fear at hearing this. Signs of panic became visible on his face. 'So, when they come again for your statement, we can organise this, unless you have some idea of where they may be,' the nurse continues.

'Oh no, no details to police please.'

'Why not?'

'They will take me back.'

'Take you back?' she asks.

'They will take me back to the detention centre.'

'Police do not put people in detention unless you have committed a crime, which is not the case here. A van hit you. Police may have the driver's details, but they will need your statement so that they can prosecute the driver, do you understand?'

'Yes, but they will lock me up. Please protect me.'

'Alright, no worries.' The nurse believes the psychologist will find the underlying cause of the problem.

'I understand you are making satisfactory progress, Mr JT,' she opens.

'Yes.'

'Mr JT, how long have you been in hospital for?' she asks.

'To be honest, I don't know. Maybe two days?'

'No worries, do you know what happened? How did you find yourself in hospital in the first place?'

'The nurse told me that a van hit me and that I was lucky to be alive.'

'Well, the good news is that soon you will be discharged. I am sure your family will be delighted to see you home. Do you have any children?'

'No, not yet.'

'A partner?'

'No.'

'Well, I could visit you then, where do you live?'

'I do not have any place to go. Please help me.'

'Okay, I will arrange for a social worker to see you,' she suggests. Dr Dami assumes that JT is a homeless person. She also believes he has sustained a brain injury and needs assistance. On these grounds, a social worker was called in.

'I understand that you know no one in this country?' Ms Benita asks. 'I am a social worker; I am here to help you. I will help you find a place to stay. I will also get a lawyer to contact the Ministry of Immigration on your behalf. So, do not worry, all will be fine. I will talk with the council to find a place where you can stay while we speak with the Ministry of Immigration. But in the meantime, I will take you home. I have a spare room where you can stay while I talk to them.'

CHAPTER 14

Two days later, JT was at Ms Benita's place in an upcoming area near the city centre in a three-bed semi on a corner plot. She has a large, fenced garden where her two children play after school. On the ground floor are two reception rooms and a kitchen rather negligible compared with other rooms. All the cooking stuff is stacked in a room initially designed to be a utility room. The boy and girl's rooms on the first floor are not different from a storage facility. There are toys all over the place. Benita's effort to keep the rooms tidy always ends in disappointment. 'I just packed all your toys; how come they are all over the place?' she keeps complaining. The children, especially K, does not want her toys packed. She needs them all the time. She has her baby doll called Bambi that sleeps with her. She turns to her when James is not playing with her. The third room that JT occupies is the smallest and, in fact, the library room. It has one corner occupied by a bookcase. Children frequently visit the room to pick a book or return one. JT felt overwhelmed by the abundance of toys and books.

As a single parent, Benita does not have any spare time. Her days are long and spread between dropping and picking up the children from school and visiting clients on a shift basis.

Although she was still in her thirties, she resembled someone in their forties.

'Let us do some shopping for you,' she says. JT did not have any spare clothes. He was easily identifiable by his rather unusual and embarrassing foreign fabrics; a multicoloured shirt with two missing buttons and a pair of trousers in a funny state. The fabrics resemble those of medieval times, and one might wonder where they were imported from. There were four large pockets on the trousers, two extremely large and zipped pockets at the back and two smaller curved pockets that have further small inside pockets making a grand total of six. 'Well, these are second-hand goods, but they are not bad. Many and even some wealthy people sometimes shop here. The thing is what you can find here could be of excellent quality and items that are now discontinued. So, they are good. Mind you, the weather is changing soon so get some jumpers, and a winter coat. You need some boots as well; they are quite handy. They keep you warm. Oops! A good blanket.'

'A room on my own? Me having a room, what I did not have in Kombi?' he was thinking.

A week, two, three passed and still no accommodation offers from the local council. But Ms Benita did not see any inconvenience, the two children, a boy and a girl were still young and could occupy one room. JT has become a good help to Benita and a new friend and a father figure for the kids. He drops and picks them up from school, a fifteen-minute journey on foot. The children were happy to tell their new friend about their day at school. JT was curious to know about children's activities in school in Western Europe. He gives his full attention to their stories and the children like that; their mother is sometimes distracted by conversations with other mothers or because of a long day at work. The new friend seems to have no pressure and shows more interest in their stories. However, sometimes JT struggled to grab the full story as he was unfamiliar with the curriculum and has limited knowledge of the culture. He realised that the kids, age seven and nine years old, were bright and knowledgeable. They could hold a conversation for longer and with a confident approach as opposed to children in Africa, who may show some signs of shyness. His new friends would fix their eyes on him and ask him direct questions; he finds this shocking and at the same time interesting. 'These children will have a brilliant future,' he thought. He keeps his answers to their questions short to avoid embarrassment. He nevertheless encourages them with a big smile and a 'yes' from time to time. The kids understood that sometimes JT did not follow their stories properly, but they were happy to talk about their day to him anyway. They feel good that at least someone is sharing their experience of the school day.

'There is a letter for you; the council has found a place for you. We will do the viewing tomorrow,' Benita informs JT.

'Good! Thanks for your help, Benita.'

'You are welcome. You have been of immense help,' she replies. 'I appreciate your taking the children to school and picking them up. I have been doing this myself and alone for quite a while and it is exhausting sometimes, especially when

I have travelled far to meet a client.' She went quiet for some seconds and looked away. JT could read the emotion on her face. "Alone" means a lot to her. She began to think about life after JT. 'So, we are going to miss you.'

A thirty-minute driving time separates Benita from JT's new destination, one of the notorious estates in the capital. Drugs and dirt welcome them before they reach the single room on the fifth floor. JT was excited that he was going to have a beautiful view of the capital being in a high-rise building. He did not note the presence of drugs on the estate. Bar its state; second-hand furniture, including a black leather couch and a TV without a remote control, a fridge with a wobbly door, a single light bulb fixed in the centre of the ceiling with deemed light, a toilet, which is right at the back of the bed, a kind of en suite, the room has a fantastic view of the capital. JT gave a big smile to Benita in approval.

'What? How can they offer you a place like this? This place is not only awful, but it is dangerous. I need to speak with the council. You deserve better than this. You can't stay here. This area has a bad reputation. Let's get out of here,' she orders.

JT tried hard to hide his disappointment. He did not want to give the impression that he was not happy to stay at Benita's, after all, she is helping him on many fronts. She is fighting his deportation case, and this is the most important thing for the time being. He nevertheless remarked that the place was not too bad, after all.

'You want trouble? Can't you see the looks of tenants here? Can't you see the way they dress?' comments Benita, to dissuade the man. She puts doubt in his mind. 'After all, I do not know this place. Benita may be right.'

'Mum is JT leaving us?' the children ask.

'No, not yet. The place is no good. It has some bad people.'

'Yes!' react the children. 'Are you happy to stay?' they ask.

'Yes, I am.'

'Can you do some shopping for us tomorrow after your school run, please, JT?' Benita asks.

'No problem. But Dr Dami wants to see me tomorrow.'

'What for? What does she want?'

'She wants to ensure that I am okay.'

'Aren't you okay?'

'Well, you know that I have my difficulties.'

'I know better than anyone else, however, she is not the right person to help you with your condition. You have PTSD.'

'What is PTSD again?' JT asks.

'Post-traumatic stress disorder. Remember, I asked you to see a psychiatrist. I will get someone to help, not her. If she is not after something else, she is after money. She is paid for her visits.'

'I understand.'

'Be careful, that is what I can say for now.'

As scheduled, Dr Dami honoured her appointment to assess JT's progress, which honestly should not be on the cards anymore. JT has fully recovered, but she feels like visiting him. There are some apparent signs that she fancies JT, although she never openly expresses it.

'Is all well with you?' Dr Dami asks.

'Yes, I am happy here,' JT replies.

'I am glad to hear that you are happy, however, I have to continue to monitor your progress to avoid nasty surprises. I also believe you need a place on your own. If you need my help, here is my card. You can call me any time. I seriously believe you need a place for your privacy; you are a man.'

'I appreciate your concerns. I will discuss with Benita.'

'I hope she will understand where I am coming from.'

'I hope so.'

JT has developed some confidence in Dr Dami. It is now with pleasure that he welcomes her. He also finds her young and attractive. He does not know why he couldn't trust her that much during their first meetings in the hospital. He now fancies her but refuses to show it. How could he possibly show it anyway? He believes that his future hangs in the hand of these two professionals, Dr Dami and Benita, the social worker. However, the fact that he now has her contact details means that he can call her from time to time, who knows?

It was noticeable that the young man was happy after he met with Dr Dami. She talks to him looking into his eyes and he could read her body language.

'What did she say,' Benita asks?

'She asked me to give her a call any time I need her. She also said that I need a place on my own.'

'What is wrong with this woman? What is she whispering? Does she mean that I am not doing enough, or has she got a hidden agenda? I will find out, I hope she is not after JT,' she pondered.

JT was becoming anxious about his immigration status. He could not work nor go to school. He was nevertheless planning his future by faith. He did not know that Benita was relentlessly working on his case. He nevertheless decided to inform his mum about his whereabouts. It has now been two good years since he left the country. 'Mum must be worried sick,' he regrettably thought.

'Bezalazur, 12th October 2002

Dear Mum,

It has been three long years in my life apart from the time I spent in the village after dropping from the studies that I cherished. I am currently in the capital city of one of Europe's respected countries. It is all well with me, I did not want to inform you about my adventure because I did not know how you were going to react, I am sorry, Mum. But I am here for you and my sisters, I know life is tough and there is no one to help you with farming, but once I settle, I will come to your rescue.

I write this note to assure you that I am alive, and you will see me one day.

Love you, Mum.

Your son,

JT.'

CHAPTER 15

The people of Kombi have a community association that meets once a month. The monthly meeting offers a platform for sharing news among the members and healing homesickness. Members of the association reconnect with their brothers and share their experiences of life in a foreign land. They remind themselves of time and weather differences. They joke about the types of clothing they wore at the time they entered the country. Some were ignorant of the wintry weather in Europe and dressed in light African fabrics. They make jokes about their early days. One of them nearly got in trouble with the police when he chased a squirrel. They also talk about their jobs and workplace. Meetings always last unnecessarily long, there has never been a formal agenda. Consequently, members talk outside the agenda to prolong the encounter. They find it difficult to end the meeting as it means returning to loneliness, especially for those who are single.

Africa means vibrance, colours, music, gathering under the shade of trees, hot food and, for some, women, and politics. Abroad, the Africans, whether in their early days or near retirement, feel some limitations in their powers and ability to enjoy themselves. They believe life is passing by as they focus on work and studies. Thus, they use any occasion to connect with the spirit of Africa and rejoice.

JT was welcomed with a big reception. The women cooked their country meals. JT was thrilled to meet the association members. 'I feel great tonight. I feel like being in Gadu. This is fantastic. I will attend the next meeting for sure. It is encouraging to hear about what they have achieved back home. It means that I can still make it. If I am patient, I will achieve my goal.'

JT was so overwhelmed that he forgot to ask for Zokoh, the man whose presence at the airport triggered his sending to a detention centre. 'Next time, I will make sure that I ask for him. From their introduction and their achievements in Kombi, I believe they all work and have good positions.'

'How was the meeting? you look so happy,' Benita enquires.

'Great! We ate our traditional meals.'

'I am sure you loved it.'

'Certainly, yes. I missed these meals.'

'I'm glad you had a wonderful time.'

The second meeting brought the joy of the country vibe. Women dressed up as if they were going to a wedding reception. Everyone wanted to hear more about JT's story as well as plans. JT was curious to hear that all the men want to go home in five to ten years. 'These people are lost; they do not know what is going on in the country. To think about returning now is incredible,' JT was thinking. However, he did not want to sound negative. He believes they may have strong reasons for willing to go back to a country still in transition. He moves the conversation to Zokoh before he forgets again. 'So, where is Zokoh?' he asks.

'Zokoh? Dr, answer our brother's question,' one of them suggests, nudging another man. 'Where did you meet him? We have not seen him for the past two years,' Dr answers with another question.

'We met at the airport. He told me that he was sent by someone to meet me.'

'This is the issue we have in our community,' Dr continues. 'Once our people get a better job, they leave us. They believe they have made it and leave the group. Since Zokoh completed his degree in computing two years ago, we have yet to set our eyes on him. I heard he now works for a bank. We are no longer the same. He has joined other communities or whatever.'

'What a shame! I was hoping to meet him again. He sounds like a gentleman.'

'Absolutely, he is a man with a good heart. We like him, but we have lost him.'

'Are you working, buddy?' one of his compatriots asks.

'Not yet, I was waiting for my paper.'

'Are you now legal in the country?'

'Yes, I am, I have got my temporary paper that permits me to work.'

'Are you not married yet with your Boottee (white woman)?'

'No, we are just friends, and she only helps me.' JT did not want to give any details.

'You are wasting time. Get married and all will go smoothly for you. I would not hesitate to take advantage had I got that chance my friend. You are too slow. Do you need a job?'

'That will be great!' JT replies.

'Can you start next week? It is a part-time job, but if you are strong you can have as many hours as you want. Talk to this man, he holds plenty of jobs,' they laugh. 'He is the "mayor" of the city, he knows everywhere and can knock on every single door in the city,' they add. 'If you work hard in this country, you can earn more than our so-called ministers back home. And you can have a better life too.'

'Yes, I am ready to start.'

JT was excited to get a job in a secondary school as a cleaner. He was shown the basic tasks to perform including table dusting, classroom sweeping and toilet cleaning. It is a two-hour job, from Monday to Friday. However, because it is a school and lessons start at 8:30 am, JT must finish his work at least fifteen minutes before the beginning of the class. JT starts at 6 am. Most of the people, including the compatriot who recruited JT, complete this task in an hour and a half. Obviously, they know the dos and don'ts. JT, on the other hand, struggles with the long and heavy broom he is given for the sweeping of the play area. That is where he spends more time. He also consumes time dusting and removing handwriting on pupils' desks.

Although commuting to work presents another challenge to the man who does not drive, JT did not mind getting up at half-past four in the morning to reach the workplace at a suitable time. He did not mind the walk; however, he was tormented by the likelihood of losing his position – the supervisor always complains about him finishing late. 'I don't want to lose my daily grind. I have been working here for fifteen years as a cleaner, and since I was appointed a supervisor five years ago, I have never seen a staff member like you. Why can't you hurry up? Next time you finish late, I will have no choice but to send you home,' the supervisor warns.

Each morning, the supervisor would visit his site at least three times. JT shook at seeing the man in his late fifties. 'If not for the sake of money would this man who looks like a ghost, tell me off every morning? He never criticises the other cleaners, only me. And the people who finish early never dust all the tables. They would dust a couple of desks here and there and that is it. I think, they only put their effort in some areas and neglect others.'

JT's problem is that he wants everything to be perfect. He cleans every single corner of the classroom, while the experienced cleaners focus on places like toilets and teachers' desks. Therefore, they have plenty of time to relax and prepare for their day jobs, some have evening jobs too. So, they reserve some energy by not spending too much time and effort on the time-consuming tasks and those that are unlikely to be checked by the supervisor. They know the tricks; they have been in the job for so long and have established trust with the supervisor. No doubt the area JT cleans looks sparkling clean. However, he does not receive any compliments for his challenging work. He only receives warnings. He always goes home with a miserable face.

JT does not only suffer low morale but also financially. Although he was overly excited to receive his first wages, because he can start rebuilding his mother's house, he realised that he was paid less for much effort. Each time he finishes work late; the supervisor deducts 1SK from his hourly rate as punishment. JT decided to confront the supervisor and was told that the next time he complains, the level of deduction will increase, he would lose 2SK instead of 1SK. JT vows to finish on time to avoid a pay cut. He wishes he could start early, but he did not have access to the site. He must wait for the supervisor who has the keys. One morning, JT reacted angrily to the supervisor's comment. The man was heard saying: 'Someone is going to lose some money this week again.' He did not mention JT's name, but clearly, the statement addresses him, given the context. JT considers this as a provocation and a step too far. He walks towards the man who looked like somebody under the influence of some substance. He grabs his collar with one hand, looks into his eyes and then punches him in the face with the other hand. The man falls flat. Other cleaners rush in to avoid the worst. Thus, JT lost his first job. He came home earlier than usual, and Benita wondered if all was well with JT.

'No,' he answers.

'What is the matter,' she asks.

'I punched the so-called supervisor in the face. He said that he did not want to see me anymore.'

'I am sorry to hear he annoyed you, but you do not use force on human beings in this country. You can be jailed for violent conduct. If you are not happy with the supervisor, you talk to the manager, but you do not fight in the workplace.'

'I'm sorry too. It is because this man really got to my nerves;

every time he walked past my area; he makes funny comments. This time, I could not control myself, I lost my temper. But I have learnt my lesson. I will not do that again.'

Having surrendered his first job, JT returned to the mayor, who sympathised with him. He nets another cleaning job, this time with a local swimming pool. It was an excellent job for JT in terms of commuting distance; only a twenty-five-minute walk from his home. It is a two-and-a-half-hour shift from 6 am to 8.30 am, six days a week. JT does not mind working Saturdays – at least he does not have to wake up at four in the morning. The supervisor, a woman in her fifties, loves him the most. She calls him 'My Sunshine.' JT has the pleasure of going to work and can outperform any other cleaner to impress the boss. It was a friendly environment. The job was also good in terms of tasks; JT mainly cleans the mirrors around the pool. He grew so rapid in the job that he could sometimes finish half an hour before the official duration of his assignments. The supervisor always thanks him when he has finished. Before he calls it a day, she would call him by his sweet name. JT likes that but sometimes he feels embarrassed.

One morning, she came and stood for a minute then storms at JT. 'What sort of cleaning is this? Look here, look. This is not done properly. Do it again. You are lucky I do not have anyone to replace you, I would have sacked you immediately.' Then she walks back to the reception desk. JT was in shock. 'What is this? I can't see anything wrong with these mirrors. They are clean. Is it not what I have been doing for some time now? I know the job. Well, if she says so, I will go over it again.'

JT left without saying goodbye to her. She did not mind either. The following morning, she greeted JT with a smile and called him Sunshine. JT wondered if it was the same woman who threatened to sack him the previous morning. The friendly atmosphere resumes for about a week. Then she stood at the same place to threaten JT with the weapon of the sack. JT liked the job and did not want to leave it. He was again spending more time and effort unnecessarily. Benita became aware of what was going on at JT's workplace. When JT comes late with a long face it means the woman has been at his back.

JT started to develop some form of phobia. He became anxious as he never knew when his good days at work would be. It was nothing to do with his performance, but the woman's humour. JT prays every morning before he goes to work, but the prayers do not change anything in the woman's unpredictable reaction. JT was thinking about looking for another job, but there was nothing he could find in his vicinity. He decides to endure the woman's harassment. Another morning, she moves again to her favourite place and stands for a minute. Before she opens her mouth, JT walks straight towards her but then remembers what Benita said. He stops short and removes his uniform. 'Here is your dirty uniform. Take your job, I do not want it anymore. I have had enough.'

'Oh no, I came to ask you for a favour.'

'I'm not interested in your favour. I am DONE.'

He walks out. The woman was in shock. She had finally decided to ask JT why he never called her by her name. She loves JT and had shown signs, but JT did not understand. JT believed he was lucky this time to have a good supervisor that never deducted his money. She used to pay him extra money for the work he did not do. She called it overtime. She smiled at him, called him my darling, my Sunshine. But all JT did was to give back a shy smile. So, she wanted to ask him if he had any reason not to approach her. However, because she stood for a second thinking about how to introduce the subject, JT concluded that she was going to have a rant again. The woman blames herself for her wrong approach. 'Perhaps I should have waited for him here at the reception to talk. Now he has gone. He believes I hate him.'

JT decides to give a call to Dr Dami, just to say hello.

'Why don't you come over for a cup of tea. There is a café near where I live. What about, say 1pm tomorrow?'

'That would be fine. See you tomorrow.'

At the café, Dr Dami orders for herself, then she asks what JT is having. JT decides to play it safe. 'Erm, the same thing please,' he says to the bar attendant.

'Ten SK please, how are you going to pay?'

JT looks at Dr Dami, thinking that she would be footing the bill. Instead, she asks if JT did not have enough cash for his order.

'Oh no, I have money on me.'

JT left the café 10SK short and in shock. 'Is she not the one that invited me? Did I tell her that I love tea so much that I wanted to put in such money? I could have sent this to my mum, and she would have blessed me. Suppose that she becomes my girlfriend or fiancée or whatever, is it how she would treat me?

Benita has never asked me to make any financial contribution whether it is towards food or bills. She understands that I do not have enough to contribute. But look at this one, she cannot offer me a simple cup of tea. How much more when we get into a relationship. We will be fighting over the sharing of house expenses. It's good that I kind of know who she is sooner rather than later. I will not tell Benita anything about this meeting.'

CHAPTER 16

Benita used the celebration of her promotion to take JT to bed. She believes it is a great opportunity to possess JT's heart or else it may be too late, and she would only have herself to blame. No one has stopped her from expressing her feelings to JT. She is convinced that one day something could happen between the two, however, the aggressive move by Dr Dami is now a threat and she is out to win JT's heart.

'JT, can you include a bottle of wine and a bottle of champagne on today's shopping list please?'

'Um, what are we celebrating?'

'You will know, I want to keep it a secret until …'

There was no doubt that Benita had recently fallen in love with JT. She has so far fought hard to hide her feelings for the man. She does not want to show that she is the one in love, it could be interpreted as a weakness. She wanted the man to take the lead. But the man is more concerned about his immigration status. Besides, he does not want to do anything silly that will affect his chance of getting his papers. Further, he has some feelings for Dr Dami. He was reflecting on having a place on his own, that could have given him the freedom to do so. Now that he lives with Benita, anything that shows signs that he loves another woman could jeopardise his chance of getting his paper, she may give up the fight with the immigration. Demanding work and raising two children have taken their toll on Benita's looks. However, with the presence of JT, she has undergone some changes. JT's help has eased pressure on her, and she has begun to take diligent care of her body. JT has noticed this and has been asking himself if he was dealing with the same woman, he met almost a year ago. He has been asking himself what could happen if this woman, who looks a little bit older than him, was to get closer. But actions from both sides sometimes give away signs of mutual attraction, only the fear of rejection keeps both camps at bay.

'Children, I got news for you. Mummy has been promoted to a senior position.'

'What does promotion mean, Mummy?' K asks.

'This means Mummy is going to bring in more money.'

'Am I going to get a games console for Christmas?' James asks.

'And a drum kit,' K jumps. K, the youngest always goes the extra mile. She loves making controlled noise. She is also full of confidence.

'A drum kits?'

'Yes, that is what I want, I promise I will not make noise.'

'Um, I am not sure about that, a drum kit that does not make noise?'

'Yes, my friend Yomy got one. Trust me, mummy, it does not make noise. I promise to be a good girl.'

'Okay, I am not promising anything for Christmas, it depends on how much I will be bringing home.'

'But Mum, you said you would be bringing more money home,' they say in unison.

'Yes, but I do not know how much yet. This was the easiest way to explain promotion to you so that you understand better, but it does not mean that Mummy is going to bring a big bag full of money home.'

'Aww,' they react in disappointment.

'How much would a drum kit and games console cost?' JT asks. 'I can make some contributions.'

'Yes!' cheer the children.

'Okay, homework time. Have you done your work? Not yet. Bring your books. It is getting late. Soon it will be bedtime.'

'Mum, can I watch TV?' K asks.

'Not before you have done your homework.'

'Okay, Mum.'

'Alright, you can now go to bed. Goodnight.'

Benita has weighed her options since the last visit of Dr Dami. She does not trust her anymore and believes she is after JT. Her frequent visits, the fact that JT has her details, who knows, after his school run, he may go and meet her. In addition, she noticed that JT was delighted to have the young lady's business card. She had asked him before about the reasons he was happy to have the lady's details and realised the man's explanation lacked cohesion. She was reading many signs that she believes show that JT is moving closer to the lady. At one point, she forced JT to cancel a scheduled meeting with Dr Dami without good reason. To cover this insecurity, she made JT help her with something that was not urgent to do in place of the meeting. From time to time, Benita warns JT about single mothers and how they can put someone in trouble, without thinking that she is also a single parent. But JT did not remind Benita that she is also talking about herself. It was about the right time to cut off Dr Dami. 'If this man leaves me for her, I will be the loser. His paperwork is making substantial progress and he may be allowed to stay in his country. I will not live to see someone else benefiting from my arduous work. Her reports on JT's mental state are working in this man's favour, but does that mean that she will take this man? I am sure if JT could choose, he will go for her. In this case, I must be quick and put an end to all speculations. No wonder he never questions me on my private life. If he had some feelings for me, I am sure he would have asked. Instead, he is more interested in why Dr Dami should be single. Does he mean that she deserves a man more than I do?'

Ms Benita sent the kids to bed early to have plenty of time for JT. She believes the celebration of her promotion will be a fantastic opportunity to have a one-to-one conversation with a man she trusts could be the person to spend the rest of her life with. She refuses to go straight to the point. Instead, alcohol was used to do the tricks.

'Bring two wine glasses for us, please. It is Friday night and I want to treat myself.'

'I am happy for you. I have never seen you in this kind of mood before; how long have you been working for them?'

'Seven years now. After my qualification, I worked for three years for a small firm in the city centre before joining them.

Let us toast to your temporary freedom, my promotion and our time together.'

'Our time together, what is she insinuating, my stay at her house or future relationship? I cannot ask now while she is at last happy today and needs to relax. Is she planning something? My last meeting with Dr Dami was cancelled for no reason. The psychologist had warned me to be careful with single mothers or else I will become a father to children I never fathered. She has also suggested that Benita is exploiting me, that I should have my own place. She said that it is my right to own a place and that she may confront Benita on this issue. I was uneasy about it in any case. The psychologist implied that Benita's attitude towards her may have some underlying jealousy. I am happy that she reminds me so that I do not make any mistakes. If anything happens now, it means that Dr Dami is out of the equation. Benita will not allow us to get any closer and I will not take any risk by going against her will. She is the one looking after me here. Who else do I really know? I kind of know Benita now. She is a good woman. She works hard and does not moan. She dedicates her time to the future of her children. And she is beautiful too. Dr Dami has already revealed her other side. I love her, no doubt about it, but I do not believe she is the person I can spend the rest of my life with, given our date.'

'Are you drinking, JT?' Benita asks.

'Yes, I'm.'

'But you have gone quiet.'

'Yes, you know that I have not drunk alcohol in almost two years. So, I have to be careful.'

'I understand. Is this taking you back to happy times in your country? Do you have anyone there?'

'Yes.'

'And you never told me?'

'Of course, I did, remember ...'

'So, who is that person?' she says, expecting to hear that JT is married or has a fiancée, which means that her plans are ruined.

'My mum and two sisters.'

'I know, what about a wife or girlfriend, or children?' She wants to make sure that JT is not a married man before she commits.

'Oh no. I do not have anyone there.'

'How come?' she asks with elation.

'I was more concerned about my future than marriage. Who is going to marry a man without a future? Everyone aspires to a better life.'

'I see. Can I have another glass please?'

'Yes, sure, why not?'

'So, are you still in touch with your psychologist?'

'Oh yes, I called her yesterday.'

'Why? What did you guys talk about?' She felt like her suspicions were being confirmed.

JT realises that he has made a blunder. However, he still has room for manoeuvre. 'Oh, I was trying to be polite. I called to apologise for cancelling the scheduled meeting on short notice. I also told her that I was getting better and that there was no real need for her to worry too much about my mental state anymore.'

'That is great,' she laughs. 'Can I have another one please?'

'I don't want to be rude, but I think you may have consumed enough alcohol already. If you continue like that, you may get drunk.'

'Who cares? I am not going anywhere. The bed is not far, and it is all I need.'

JT checks the clock, and it is past midnight. This was unusual for Benita. She normally gets to bed after the children. JT was frequently checking the clock to signal to Benita that it was getting late, but Benita was talking nonstop. 'Come on Benita, it is getting late, let's go to bed.'

But Benita could not stand on her feet. JT helped her as much as he could. He helped her reach her bedroom. She could not push the door, so JT did it for her. He put her in bed, but she hung on to him and brought him down. 'Don't go yet, give me my gown and please help me with my belt.'

JT hesitated. 'How can I possibly undo a woman's belt?' He nevertheless obeyed.

'My shoes, please! Please help me sleep.' JT laid by her side, and they spent the night they had waited for together.

The children ran to JT's room early in the morning the next day as they always do before breakfast, but JT was not there. 'Mummy, JT is not in his room.'

'Yes, I know, he is here to help Mummy. Mummy cannot stand on her feet.' They both laughed and went to the dining room.

Three months later, JT receives a letter from his mother.

'Dag, District Dan City, 7 December 2002,

My dear son,

I trust the God we serve. I know that He will spare your life, He will always protect you. For the past two years, I have been praying for you. There were times I could not eat. I did not have any appetite. Some wicked tongues have preached your death, but I believe in a living God. Others have said that you had rejected your home. They are saying that you are now married to a foreign woman, and you have children and you do not want anyone to know about it and for that reason, you were hiding. How can I communicate with my grandchildren who do not speak our language? Do not forget Fay-Fay. She is a diligent woman and comes here regularly to help me. She is a God-fearing woman. She is from a good family, and I would love her to become a part of our family too. How would I know that the one you have married is from a good family? You have forgotten our tradition.

What food do you eat there, my son? Are you eating well, son? Please do not go hungry. A man shall eat well in the morning before he goes out so that he is strong among his fellow men. You are far from me, and it has been so long that you have not eaten your favourite sauce. Do you eat our food there? Do you know where to get it there? Please tell me so that I can send you some of our food. As you know, I always keep some for you. I miss you, my dear son. When are you coming home? You know that I am getting old. Please come home before I die.

My house is near collapse. Please think about it. Next year, I would like to move northward and farm our family land that the neighbours are claiming. I will continue to farm, but you know that I am now becoming weak. If not for Fay-Fay, I would find it difficult doing any demanding work by myself now. Find a nice present for her, my son.

Love,

Mama.'

JT regrets writing at a time he is unable to help. It would have been better if he did not know that things were not well with Mum. 'She wants her house repaired. She wants to see me now. How can I travel without a travel document? I cannot leave this place. I am still a potential prisoner; I have surrendered my passport. She said she is weak and old, what would I do if she dies now? For sure people are mocking Mum, but God is great. Once the fight is over, I will look after Mum.'

CHAPTER 17

The children have observed that JT is now regularly in Mummy's bedroom. Before they ask, Benita weaves an alibi. 'Mummy now needs JT's help either for massage or moving stuff around in the bedroom,' she says, but did not get any reply from the children. Benita was concerned about the children's reaction to her relationship with JT. Their father, KF, a drunkard and former serviceman visit them from time to time. Although his conditions have deteriorated to the extent that he has not seen his children for the past twelve months, he nevertheless remains their father and they sometimes ask her about their father's visit, or absence rather. Benita held back on telling the children the truth. Fortunately, they seem to have accepted JT so far. There is a fifty-fifty chance that they may be in favour of Mummy getting another man. So, three months into the relationship, Benita decided to give some hints. 'Children, I've got news for you.'

'I know,' K says.

'What is it?' Benita asks.

'Mummy is going to bring more money home and I am going to get my drum kit.'

'You got it wrong, my dear. Think hard! It is not about

promotion this time, it's something else and I doubt you will guess it right.'

'Oh, I think, I know,' claims James. 'JT got a new place.'

'Not quite right, it's something to do with JT, but not moving to a new house. However, you were close, son, JT is moving room. Mummy does not want to call him every morning for help. So, he is going to stay in Mummy's room to make Mummy's life easier.'

'So, can I move to his room?' K asks.

'Not yet, when the time is right, I will let you know.'

'Okay, Mum.'

The charity 'Veterans' Lives Matter' has been working hard to improve the living conditions of former servicemen. KF has been taking his drugs regularly and now he is having some quiet nights. Nightmares keep him awake most of the time. To be able to sleep, he had resorted to heavy drinking, but things have been different recently. 'I think I should go and see the kids this week, it has been a while,' KF projected.

'You cannot just pop up like that without warning me, darling,' reacted Benita as KF rang the bell.

'I am sorry, but I felt like seeing the kids.'

'Okay come in, they will not be long. They are at school. How is life with you?'

'Not bad, I feel much better.'

'That is great, I'm glad to hear things are improving.'

'And you?'

'We are okay.'

'I want to come back home.'

'You what? Come back? No chance! How many years since you left this place? Why are you asking for permission? Are you not the one who voluntarily left this place? Anyway, it is too late. You broke my heart, and I am now recovering. So, let us not get into the past. You are here to see our children, period – unless you do not want to see them.'

'Hey, Dad is here!' interject the children. They had not seen him for an exceptionally long time. But the excitement was not the same having now been used to a stranger who is becoming their stepfather. JT treats them well and they are happy with him.

'I understand your reaction, Benita. Who is this man?'

'My friend.' Benita did not want a violent reaction by KF to cause embarrassment that could lead to something else.

'A friend? Since when? And what has he got to do with my children?'

'Our children.'

'Our children, whatever you call it, he should stay away from them. What sort of friend is that? Boyfriend?'

'What is your problem? Boyfriend or not, it is not your business.'

'Of course, it is not my business, but I'm sure you are having an affair with this poor man. Look at him.'

'Don't talk like that. This man is my new boyfriend, and as matter of fact, we are getting married if you want to know more. He has put joy in my heart. I have decided to marry him. You left my life in limbo with two kids to raise. Are you not ashamed of yourself? You destroyed my future, the future of my children and your future too. Shameful man, why don't you get another wife? I have a man who cares about me and my children, not someone like you who abandons his family.' A moment of silence follows. His memories went back to their best times as spouses. He regretted leaving home at the time Benita most needed his help with raising the children. He could read her pain as a pseudo-single parent in a city like Bezalazur where life is lived almost in the fast lane.

'I know, I let you down, but you could get someone else, not some random immigrant. These immigrants are smart. They come here and seduce vulnerable women just to get papers.'

'Mind your language.'

'I won't, can you not see this man? Clearly, he is younger than you. Do you think he loves you? He is after papers. I am sure you are an undocumented immigrant. I will shoot your plan down. Trust me,' pointing his finger at JT.

Doors slammed behind him as he left in frustration, furious about his former concubine falling in love with another man. Alcohol and war trauma has seriously affected his physical appearance. 'I will destroy this man's hope,' he vowed. JT was visibly troubled by the scene he saw. But Benita assured him that nothing will change in their relationship. Yet JT could not sleep, is Benita telling him the truth? Would her ex come back and harm him? Has he got the power to destroy his dream? Who knows, he may have some connection with the police or immigration? The future now looks bleak after the incident.

The following day, the children come to their mum to find out more about her future with the stranger. 'Mummy, when are you getting married?' K asks.

'I don't know the date yet.'

'Is Daddy coming to your wedding,' they ask.

'I am not sure, I doubt it. Why?'

'I think, he is not happy,' replies K.

'I know, such is life.'

'Do you have a plan, Mummy? Who are the flower girls?' K asks.

'Well, I don't know yet. I do not have a plan yet.'

'I can help you, Mum,' volunteers K.

'Oh yes, I know you can help. You are good at planning things, aren't you? Have you planned your homework?'

'Yes, I will do my homework after my program.'

JT took his fellow Africans' advice and pushed for marriage. 'It would facilitate the paperwork,' he argues. Benita did not see any inconvenience as this would mean that Dr Dami is out of the picture. Although the wedding was announced at short notice, parents who drop their children at school welcome the news. JT has won so many hearts in the community and beyond. He always smiles, even at people he meets for the very first time. He does not walk past anyone in the street without greeting them. His mother taught him to be kind to strangers because not all humans are human beings; some could be God incarnate. 'Would you walk past your maker without greeting him?' she always says. He was also popular among the congregants at his local church. Those who know him and those who simply heard about him got together to make his special day a memorable one. A large reception room was hired for the occasion. People came from all over the capital and beyond.

On the wedding day, the civic centre had to turn people away because of lack of capacity. Many people decided to go to the reception hall because they could not find a seat in the town hall. As the officer calls the name of the groom and bride, two immigration officers enter the room. 'Hold on, officer, we need to proceed to a random check please. This is a routine check. We are immigration officers.'

At the name of immigration, the room plunges into a deep silence. One by one, foreigners who did not have their papers in order and those with temporary papers begin to slip out of the room. By the time the officers introduce themselves, half the invitees had vanished. Those who could jump the wall did it swiftly. Women abandoned high heel shoes. 'This is a burden; I cannot run fast with high heel shoes. I would rather lose them and be out of sight than face immigration officers. They have been deporting people in large numbers recently and I do not want problems. And this skirt annoys me; I cannot spread my legs enough and run fast. Why did I wear African attire in the first place? I would have vanished among the men over there who had worn simple shirts with trousers,' some women were thinking. In the corner of the street by the main entrance of the town hall was parked a van to welcome them. The immigration officers had occupied the four corners of the centre. 'Hello sirs, hello madams, can you produce any proof of ID please?' the officers ask.

'We are coming from a wedding,' they answer in a group.

'Yes, we know, but we want to know that you have the right to stay in this country.'

It is general panic, some ran back, but there were officers there as well. At the front, ID controls were taking place. Some went hiding at the back of the building but were still visible with their African attires. Some women remove their scarves while other men try to hide their long robes and black-yellow and white boubous unsuccessfully in their handbags. Cars were abandoned for a shortcut behind a garage. Seven among them were taken to police custody facing deportation. Sweat starts to run from JT's forehead. He thought he was free by now, but the arrival of immigration officers was a twist he never hoped to experience again. The fear of a return to jail came to his mind.

'Go ahead,' the officer says.

'Sir, can you confirm your address for us please?' an immigration officer asks JT.

'Twenty-three Avenue Road. Upper District.'

'Can we see a photo ID please?'

'I don't have one.'

'Any other proof of ID.'

'No.'

'Follow us please.'

'What? You can't spoil my day, officers. Since when do we carry ID to weddings? This is not right. I am a citizen, where is the problem?' screams Benita.

'Madam, we got nothing to do with you. Since this man cannot show any ID for us to check his immigration status, we can't allow the ceremony to proceed. We are sorry but we are only doing our job. There are so many bogus marriages taking place in this country and the government has instructed us to check the immigration status of foreigners who get married here. He will come back when he proves he has the right to remain.'

People who have taken time off work and have invested in the ceremony clearly were unimpressed. They could not believe immigration could spoil their party like that. 'This action will cost you dearly. I will take legal action against your office. You cannot ruin our day and go free, no way. You do not have any right to do this. Show me a search warrant. You people separate families,' the nuptial family voices in disgust.

'The party is cancelled,' someone announces to those who went straight to the reception room. 'The immigration officers have stopped the wedding. I am sorry,' he says. 'The bridegroom has been taken to an unknown destination. So, I'll update you in due course. In the meantime, you can go home because no one knows when he will be back.'

'We will hang around for at least an hour in case they release him early,' voices the public in support.

CHAPTER 18

Incidentally, JT is taken back to Camp X and a member of the kitchen staff recognises him. 'You have been here before, haven't you?'

'Nope,' he replies. 'I may resemble somebody who has been here, but I have never stepped foot in this prison before.'

'Hello, welcome back Mr "I don't like this". What brings you back this time?' asks another one.

'Yes, they got me again,' he replies.

'How?'

'To cut the long story short, they checked me out at a wedding ceremony.'

'What a shame,' the man sympathises with him. 'If you're illegal in this country, don't go to dodgy wedding ceremonies. Getting married to European citizens to remain in this country has become a booming business and authorities have their eyes on these ceremonies. There is big money involved in this business. Some people pay up to five thousand DSK to a wife-to-be that they have never met before and don't even know. If you are patient, you can get your papers legally in this country. In my case, I had to wait for ten years before I was permitted to stay. So be patient. Avoid being on their radar and they will ignore you.'

'Thank you for your advice.'

Away from family, JT became depressed. He could not work out what was going on in his life. He believes all is lost and life does not have any meaning anymore. Worse, Zana has left the camp. He did not have anyone to relate to. New anxious faces emerge in the camp, although routine remains the same. Nights were now too long for JT. He could no longer see the children in the morning. The fear of deportation increases as he has now more to lose – the wife, the children, and a life full of promise. Like Zana, JT stops talking to people for no reason. He also skips meals. He was condemned to a monotonous cycle of sunrises, sunsets and staring into the distance. Some kitchen staff who knew him became concerned about his condition. 'Surely, this man must be missing his loved ones. He is different from the man that was here before.'

Petitions were flying to the Ministry of Interior to free JT from detention, from the children's school to the local priest and Amnesty International. K and James were also actively engaged in the campaign to bring back their stepfather to be. They took a step further in their quest to mount pressure on the ministry and speed up JT's release.

Letters to the Ministry of Interior. K writes:

'Dear Madam,

I think this man should stay for multiple reasons. Firstly, he takes care of us very well and he is the most careful person I know. Secondly, we do not want him to go to the centre that is like a jail for just coming somewhere that is not his country. Thirdly, we all have rights, and we all know that. Fourthly, he helps all of us.

Yours Sincerely.'

James writes:

'Dear Madam,

I honestly think that he should not leave. He has taken care of us like bathing us, feeding us, and dressing us. People should be able to live anywhere. Just because he comes from, for example, Africa does not mean he has to live in Africa. It is called 'FREEDOM'.

Yours sincerely.'

JT was no longer fighting alone. He now has a large family of friends and simple acquaintances with him, and the 'Set JT Free' movement was growing steadily. His confidence grew and he now faces daily challenges at the centre with some optimism. 'Surely the minister of immigration will not ignore the will of thousands of people. The minister will have compassion on me; I do not envisage him ignoring these petitions. He may consider the movement behind my case to make the right decision, meaning a favourable decision to avoid hurting many people and particularly the feelings of his own people. Human rights are respected in this country. I have suffered enough. More than three years in this country and I am still between freedom and infringement. What is my sin? Is it a crime to love someone? I am now in love with Benita, and she is pregnant with our first child. To send me back means that I will never see my baby. He should think about it and have compassion. A child needs a father, I mean both parents.

'Right, gentlemen, come with me,' a security guard orders. 'If you are from Kombi, on my right; Maputa, on my left …

in front of me. Now each one of you is going to sing for me a popular song from his country. You must also exhibit the steps. Think about what you are going to sing, and how people dance in your country. Is that clear?'

'Yes,' they reply.

JT was going through a long repertoire of his country music. However, music is not his favourite subject. He had always criticised musicians. He believes musicians are lazy people who do not make any effort to contribute to the development of Africa. He values science more than anything else. For him, musicians have an easy life; they dress up and live a lavish life while scientists use their brains to create things that will improve the quality of life. They dress funny and make noise. Some have funny haircuts. But the real issue is that, for JT, Africa has danced enough and should get back to real life, which is producing goods or manufacturing. He overlooks the importance of arts and music in society. Now he must sing and dance. 'Why is this guard asking us to sing and dance? Does he want to ensure that where we say we are from is truly our place of birth or just to humiliate somebody? Whatever the case may be, does it mean that music is so important? I think I can manage a song of a musician from my region. Although I have never sung, and danced, at least I know the lyrics.'

JT was shaking. Some people were ordered to sing properly or dance well. It is funny and a bit entertaining for some detainees who have lovely singing voices. The experience can turn out to be humiliating sometimes for those like JT who are shy and cannot sing, but it was bringing life to the camp. One by one they perform, to the pleasure of the guard.

'Your turn, sir,' pointing at JT. He has been moving back each time, unfortunately, there is no one left to perform. He is the last person. As JT opens his mouth, all the detainees present, became silent. JT's mental health has been deteriorating in recent days and they did not want to add insult to injury. 'Are you from XZ's country?' the guard asks.

'Yes, I am.'

'I used to listen to his songs. I absolutely adore his music. So, tell me more about him. What's the meaning of the song?'

The guard was disappointed that JT could not hit the notes right. He nevertheless appreciated JT's effort to revive his memories. He was satisfied to get the meanings of the song but could not afford to ask JT to repeat it, knowing JT's weakness.

JT felt the weight of humiliation. Some brave men in the camp ironically hailed him as the best singer. He was thinking whether to tackle the guard one day as a way of getting his own back.

Some detainees have developed mental illness here already. Many are angry about time wasted in detention, which will never be recovered, and that brings frustration.

'What sort of life can someone who has been so traumatised live? Look at these young people who leave their country for the very first time being put in prison in a foreign land. Who is here to take them out? Further, we do not know the length of our stay in darkness. What is our crime? Seeking to better our lives? This experience is agonising. I believe this country does not want us, that is why they treat us like criminals, and this scar will remain with us forever. If I become a citizen after a long battle, I will set up a group to lobby the government. The group's objective will be to bail out immigrants. It will be our responsibility to care for them. This will give them a pleasant experience even if at the end of the day they are sent back. We will prepare their repatriation. The group will also defend the right of the immigrants. We will lobby the government to pass legislation that will prohibit detention except for a short stay at the airport. I suppose Tetnov lives by human rights, however, this does not apply to outsiders and those seeking to enter the country, I believe. But the government in Tetnov pays little attention to human rights abuse in detention centres. The people who do the dirty job of removals are private organisations. In that sense the government has clean hands', JT was thinking.

Ms Benita was reflecting on who could have possibly drawn the attention of immigration to her wedding. Her former partner, although aware of her intention to wed an undocumented immigrant, did not know the date of the ceremony. So, who else if not Dr Dami? How could she have been informed? Was JT still in contact with her? Did he inform her about their relationship? Why would he do that? Surely the neighbourhood is too good to report to the Ministry of Interior about an illegal immigrant in their ward. It must be Dr Dami and Benita was going to pour her anger out on her.

'Hello, Madam!'

'Who is calling?'

'I am Benita, Mr JT's guardian.'

'Afternoon, Mrs JT.'

'How do you know about our marriage?'

'A little bird told me.'

'Why did you not come to the wedding then?'

'Why should I? You did not want me to get any nearer to your dear JT. Why should I bother? You got him, good luck! Period! Did you invite me?'

'I see, I now know who is behind the immigration raid at our wedding.'

'Well, you know that you cannot wed an undocumented immigrant. Is there any way I can help? I have been trying to locate him unsuccessfully.'

'Aren't you happy? Why do you want to know his whereabouts? Are you not the one who masterminded evil plans for his deportation? Why did you not say that you love him? You could have him, but you chose to send him home. Trust me, he will get out. And when he does, stay away from him. I do not want to see your shadow in my life. You evil woman, no wonder why you are still single. Go and look for another man. If you think he is going to be deported, you are deceiving yourself. I will ensure that he stays, and we will have the most memorable wedding in this city. Trust me. If you try again, you will meet me.'

CHAPTER 19

It has been six long and agonising months for Benita. Sending JT to the detention centre has also sent Benita back to her old routine; she is back to dropping and collecting the kids from school, a duty that had been relegated to JT. She is also back to weekly shopping and other tasks including ironing children's clothes on Sundays. There is no one to share her daily frustrating and depressing stories with. Like the children, she feels the absence of the man in the house. Learning that her presumed rival was behind the raid by the immigration officers at her wedding made things worse. She vows to get her back once JT is out. Long nights of preparing petitions to lobby the government seem to have the best of Benita again. She is genuinely concerned about the fate of her lover and the father of her third child. The children have been asking their mother about when JT will be back. They could not understand the meaning of detention nor why someone could be detained for entering another country. They believe they could just call him and ask him to come home. The atmosphere at the school gate has changed with the absence of JT. Although some parents were happy to see Benita back, most have expressed their compassion for her misadventure with a stranger. Some blame her for rushing into the relationship. Others believe she did the right thing. Benita was inundated by the ongoing support of a local campaign group for the release of her boyfriend.

At a quarter to four in the morning, four security guards stormed JT's cell. Without asking for their ID number this time, they took the four of them to a white van outside the gate. It was a massive removal plan across the country. Twenty-six inmates were coming from other detention centres to make it thirty for a charter flight to Africa. Among the deportees were a student who overstayed his visa, a man in his forties who had been trafficked into the country at the age of nine years old and had lived all his life here, a father of seven who had been in prison for three years for an unknown offence and a drug dealer who has now become mentally unstable. It was winter and bloody cold at the airport. It was also dark, and JT was confused about the setting this time. It was not a normal flight; it was just for the detainees. 'This time, I am going home. That's the end of the road for me; an unfulfilled dream.' Although the mercury was at minus five, large drops of water were coming from JT's forehead. His heart was beating too fast. His sweater was already damp. He gets more agitated by the thought that he would not assist the birth of his first child, nor see him or her. He is also going to miss his two stepchildren. He has become their father and they were close to his heart. They could not go to sleep without saying goodnight to him. They always tell him the story of their day at school. If a friend has been nasty to them, they would tell him. He always had some wise words for them: 'Don't worry, tomorrow will be better,' he would tell them. The other passengers wondered whether JT was under the influence of some substance. 'Can someone sweat at this time of the year?' they were asking themselves. At 5.45 am, a representative of the Ministry of Immigration got on the plane for a final check. He proceeds to the headcount followed by name calling. As he moved down the carriage, a man stood up and in a loud voice said: 'Man dies once, you cannot separate family and go free. If I must die, we will die together. Yes, we must die together. This man must travel with us.' Some detainees blocked the door. While the crew captain was trying to calm them down, he saw someone waving papers. 'Hold on! Hold on!' he was heard saying. He ran to the aircraft and handed in a letter of injunction to the crew captain. 'Gentlemen, I have got news for you.' No one was interested in listening to the flight captain. They were busy dealing with the representative of the Ministry of Interior. Someone tackled him down. The flight captain cut the engine off. 'Listen, gentlemen, I have some good news for you, the flight is called off.' A minute of silence follows, then a huge 'hooray!' from the thirty detainees in unison. All thirty 'prisoners' were freed. They walked past the man they had attempted to take hostage without noticing his presence. In the early hours, newspapers published news of the failed deportation case to Africa. The headline read 'Last-minute legal battle ditches a charter flight with criminals on board.' The lawyers had been fighting with the Ministry of Interior over the case of the then human trafficking victim and the man who spent years in prison for a crime he did not commit. Shortly before midnight, a judge granted the lawyer's injunction to halt the scheduled deportation.

JT was unaware of the legal battle valiantly and relentlessly fought by the two men's lawyers. He was confused when they were told to go home. He thought that they would be going back to the 'prison cell'.

'Where do I go?' he asks the lawyer.

'Where do you want to go? You want to go to Africa?' he asks JT.

'No,' JT replies.

'You are free, go home.'

JT fell at his feet. 'Thank you, sir! God bless you, sir! You are my saviour! God bless you mightily!'

'You are welcome! Just go home,' the lawyer says.

JT's second spell at the detention centre was unpleasant and he is now mentally unstable. Hence, although delighted to be freed again, he was confused about the next step. He did not call Benita to come and collect him nor arrange for transportation. He was wandering at the airport going from shop to shop without purchasing anything. In his confusion, he became a hero. When the first news reporters arrived at the airport, JT was still at the waiting hall announcing his escape to whoever was ready to listen to him. He was interviewed alongside the defendants' lawyer.

'Mummy! Mummy!' K calls her mother. 'Daddy is talking to journalists on Tele', she said. 'What do you mean Daddy talking on Tele? Your Daddy is in a secure place and not allowed to speak to journalists. Get ready for school, time is running.'

'Please come Mummy.'

Benita couldn't believe her eyes. 'What's going on?'

'My flight has been cancelled for some irregularities and I

want to make sure people and especially my family knows that I'm once more a free man', he said to journalists.

'What are your plans? Are you going to sue the airline?'

'What for?' he asks.

'For compensation; wasting your time.'

'I don't need that. I just want to be with my family.'

'Do you want to say something to them?'

'Yes, when I see them.'

'You can talk to them now. They will see you and hear.'

'I don't know where they are.'

'Are they not in this country? Which part of the country are they in?'

'I don't know.'

'You can't remember your own address anymore? Do you remember your children of wife name?'

'Yes, but I don't know how I got here.'

'Bloody hell! This man is confused. I need to collect him. Children, you follow the neighbours to school today. I need to go to the airport now,' she said.

CHAPTER 20

Although JT has been freed by the de facto deportation injunction, he must face the Immigration Appeal Court to get his citizenship. JT was confident that he would win the battle. He has the support of local people. The children had written to the minister in charge for the return of their stepfather. Human rights campaign groups had lobbied the government to make concessions.

Benita believes JT should get a new lawyer to defend her husband-to-be.

'I am happy to represent you,' says the new lawyer. 'We need to prepare your file. Are you in touch with your former lawyer?'

'No, sir. Since the refusal letter from the Ministry of Interior, he has refused to take my calls. My calls no longer go beyond the reception. I personally believe that the secretary has received instructions to bar my calls. She always says that the man is in a meeting or with clients and will call me back, he never calls back. So, I don't know.'

'What I need from you is a couple of papers from your country that support your case. I need a paper that discloses your political activities. I need a paper with your photo at a political rally. I also need a membership card for your political party. Can you also supply me with a paper that shows that the government is hunting you down? All this will make the case stronger.'

JT had a problem. 'Who is going to collect all the papers the lawyer is asking for? What is he going to tell them? Why does he need all these papers? Where are the people going to find those papers in the first place? They do not archive newspapers.' He does not want people to raise suspicion on his stay in Europe. 'What is this man preparing for his own country, is he involved in politics?' his people may think. 'Is he preparing a coup d'état?' People over there are ignorant about the asylum system, they are familiar with coup d'états. So, it is a dilemma for JT.

'How are we going to solve the business of journals from Kombi?' JT asks Benita.

'Did you not say that you have people down there?'

'Yes, but I do not want people to know I am a beggar in this country. Africans are fussy about what they do. They cannot realise that this is not my country and that I must do what it takes to survive. But people are in general ignorant about asylum and how it works. In addition, I am officially dead in the country, which the lawyer does not know. If the national newsroom has some archives, it would be on Detective JT, but you don't want that, absolutely not. So maybe it would be safer to tell him that we cannot access any paper from back home.'

'I know what to do, what about visiting the local library? We could try and talk with some Africans who have lived here long enough and have access to African newspapers. They may direct us.'

Six months later, JT is in the Immigration Appeal Court. Like at the failed wedding, friends of the family came early to the hearing and in numbers. They stood together outside the court to fight for justice. 'This man should be allowed to stay in this country, we need people who can lift our community spirit like him,' a man commented. 'Some immigrants enter this country without checks and commit horrible crimes. Those who have proved to be genuine like this humble man should be accepted,' he continues. Some members of the group hold placard that read 'We love JT', 'Justice for JT', 'We need JT' …

'Are all your witnesses present?' the adjudicator asks.

'Yes, sir.'

'Is the representative of the Ministry of Interior ready for questioning?'

'Yes, sir.'

'Before we proceed, may I ask the witness bench to introduce itself,' the adjudicator suggests. 'From left to right, please,' he advises.

JJ Prince, Head of School, Pinchy.

Reverend J S, St Palm Church, Pinchy.

Deacon Priestley, Pinchy.

Archdeacon Paula Ashley Northeast Diocese.

Bishop Andrew, Northeast Diocese.

Outside the supporters hold hands in prayer so that all goes well inside. They pray that the judge is lenient with their man.

'Can I have a quick word with you please, sir?' the adjudicator addresses the Ministry of Interior's representative. 'Honestly, I cannot proceed with the presence of a bishop on the witness bench. I think we should just close this case.'

'Why can't we continue?'

'Who am I to scrutinise a bishop? Also, I believe this man must be a good man to have such support. We need such people in our community, not criminals.'

'I understand, but I have to do my job.'

'Well, you can do your job for the same outcome. I'm going to grant him the right to remain.'

'So, what do I tell my boss?'

'Leave it with me.'

'Okay, go ahead.'

'Honourable Bishop Andrew, I am going to make a decision. I cannot waste your time. I consider this matter closed. I will write to Mr JT tomorrow. Nothing to worry about, he can celebrate his victory. I will write to confirm my decision. Children, you can go home with your dad.'

In one accord, 'Thank you, Mr Judge, you are a good man. You have answered our prayers. May God bless your career.' It was jubilation outside as the first witness emerged to announce victory, not commiserations like on the wedding day. This time the party must go on.

CHAPTER 21

With liberty comes pressure to do more and better. JT can work and study as he wishes. However, time is not on his side and such a genius must do his best to reach his goals; can he study medicine at his age? It is unlikely; nursing was still an option. JT is aware that his mother is getting old and will need financial support. Her living conditions are deteriorating in the absence of her son. Hence JT believes his best take would be to combine work with studies. Many in his African community have done it and so could he. 'It may be a way of killing two birds with one stone; I will not go skinny while I prepare for my degree in nursing. The best approach would be to work at night and study during the day. Sleep can wait!' Luckily, the man nicknamed 'the mayor' in JT's community association still has jobs to spare.

'Can you stay awake all night?' the man asks JT.

'I can try. Why not?' JT replies.

'Have you consulted your Boottee?'

'I believe, she would not mind.'

'Here is the address. The job starts at twenty-two hours and finishes at five am.' Association members look at JT and laugh, thinking he would find the hours challenging.

'Alright, thank you,' JT collected the address without further comment.

On paper, the job sounds straightforward, to pick litter on trains and dust the cabin. Each cleaner has six trains to clean before five in the morning, the time transport service resumes in the capital. There were seven metro lines from the eastern train depot. Three of the seven lines have clean trains, but the remaining, and especially the busy central Bezalazur trains, are very dirty. Whoever cleans the inner-city train has the busiest night. JT was privileged to only clean inner-city trains occasionally. The reason: the supervisor loves football and knows all the great footballers on the continent. He is one of the fans of BB Sol. In one of his comments of the weekend matches, he mentioned BB Sol's ninety-minute goal. JT was proud to tell him that BB Sol was from his country. From that night the supervisor connected to JT, and he favoured him. Occasionally, he assigns JT an inner-city train to avoid complaints by other cleaners. He purposely does this on weekends when the inner trains are less foul since offices are closed in general on weekends. The other cleaners know that JT is the boss's favourite, but do not mind too much, such is life, they conclude.

There was a cleaner called Bell that annoyed JT in his early days. He behaves like a diplomat. He talks like a great leader. He is arrogant. He sounds like one of those African dictators. He was always right. He always blabbers on, even inside the bathroom designed for those who want to change their clothes before they go home. JT found his attitude abhorrent but at the same time waggish. There was another thing that JT found repulsive about Bell; he always comes late for the 2 am break with a fish-based meal. It is not the meal or the fish that is the problem, but the smell of the fish. No one knows if the fish he ate was in date. Before he even pulls out his meal, JT always covers his nose. And he never varies his diet, same fish, same smell every single night. JT wishes he could just go back to cleaning his train, but he needs some rest. 'Should I tell this man off? What could possibly be his reaction. Is there any way I can bar him from polluting this place with a nasty fish smell? Dialogue may work,' JT thought.

'Bell, what is your educational background? You talk like a man in command,' JT asks.

'Oho, yeah, don't you know that I am the next president of Zante in east Africa?' Bell replies.

'That is what he has been singing to our ears for the past three years,' the other cleaners obtrude in unison. 'We can't wait to serve in his government. At least he is one of us, and he will offer us a good ministerial post,' they add sarcastically.

'Look at how people with little faith react. Disoriented fellows with no yearning. I do not blame you; the longer you stay in this place the more inverted you become. You are deluded by the little money you earn in this place and have unredeemed your dreams. Rather than raising your spirit, you have chosen to raise your muscles. There is no fire left in your belly; callowness has taken over. If it is what you people think, then think again. I want exceptional people with drive and purpose. What would you people bring to the table? Do you have connections? Who are your friends in this country? I want to bring change to east Africa. You think I am joking?' He poses for a second and laughs. 'Sorry, JT, I am in my final year of a master's in international relations. I am a diplomat.'

JT's views suddenly change on the man. 'Can you tell me more about the course?'

'What I can tell you right now is that we meet VIPs. I have some great connections and have met great men in this world. That is why I am full of confidence.'

JT fell in love with Bell. He wished he had enrolled on the same course; this would have allowed him to meet great men as well. As a qualified nurse, the prospect of meeting even a local governor is very slim. He became friends with Bell and accepted to swallow the smell of fish every night; the price to pay to hear stories about great men. JT was always happy to go to work and hear about stories from unverified sources from the man with a dominating voice. Only cleaning trains on weekends was not pleasant in any form. The trains are seriously dirty and particularly the coaches towards the end. Food, drink, and other litter that can make somebody sick can be found on at least four of the ten coaches. It is recommended that cleaners wear face masks to clean the train, but this does not stop the strong smell of alcohol and something that JT could not identify.

One night, JT put his hand on something soft and cold. He dropped it and stood back. He tried again to put it in his litter bag but discovered something the author refuses to describe graphically here. It looks like some drunkard has eased himself in a paper on coach number eight. He moved to coach number nine that looks like a gent's toilet. He runs to coach number ten, which was not different from a ladies' toilet. He jumped out of the coach suffocated since he had been holding his breath inside to control the strong odour. He called the supervisor to assess the state of his train. 'Sorry JT, it happens sometimes. You have been lucky to receive clean trains. I inspect trains before I allocate them to cleaners. I have tried to give you the easiest ones each time. However, today I was tired and could not inspect all the trains. Well, it is good, at least you will be aware of what other cleaners face every week. Sorry, my dear friend.'

JT weighs his options. He considers calling it a day. However, leaving that job, which allows him to send some money for the building of his mum's house, would lead to financial hardship and 'the mayor' may not trust him with work again. He has already lost two jobs and does not want to lose this one too. In this job, he does not have any problem with the supervisor. He never works the full six hours due to the fact he always cleans the light trains. But what was in the last three coaches of the train to clean tonight was beyond his abilities. He was not well equipped to clean the equivalent of three large bedrooms transformed into three 'toilets'. JT had to clean his own mess as he felt sick before cleaning others. 'Is this what "the mayor" has been doing for the past seven years? Does he see things like this every weekend? How can somebody go through things like this and give the money later to someone else? This is hard. How many times am I going to face such a challenge?' JT refuses to eat his breakfast the following morning.

'What is wrong with you, my dear?' the wife asks.

'Oh no, I can't describe what I saw last night. It makes me sick. And guess what I put my right-hand in. How can I use this hand to eat now?'

'Well use your left hand to eat then,' she laughs.

'And the film?'

'Forget about the film.'

'That is the point. It is because of the film that I can eat. It is "here" right now. And I also used my left hand in the following coach. So, I can't eat.'

Moving on, JT became cautious about how he dealt with what looked like parcels on trains. He hates the two metro lines that bring dirty trains. He also hates working weekends. Dealing with strong smells and cleaning human mess became a weekend routine. And JT remembers the advice Sergeant, the fellow from the church in Africa, gave him. He must study to get out of these types of jobs. The jobs gave him the money he needed to support his siblings in Africa, but at what price? Healthwise, JT was feeling sick every Sunday, having faced the weekend challenge on the last coaches of the train.

CHAPTER 22

Benita's input was regularly required in the second year of JT's course. He struggled to read his own handwriting. Combining studies with a night job was looking like climbing a mountain. Long zigzags and crosses appeared in his notebook instead of handwriting. For his revision, every so often he calls for Benita's help: 'Darling, what is this word here?' pointing at some scribbles in his notebook.

'How am supposed to know? Was I there? Are you not the one who took these notes? You crossed out some words and asked me to read.'

'I did not cross these words, you don't understand. I dozed off and the pen slipped on the page.'

'But darling, you have these heavy lines on almost all pages of your notebook, can you not try?'

'How can I? Anyway, this is not the point. What is this word?'

'I can't read. You see, your spelling is so poor that it is difficult to make sense of any word here. Your handwriting resembles hieroglyphs.'

'Oh no, you are going too far.'

'Alright, sorry. What do you do to keep awake?'

'I dream about you.'

'Not in the classroom. You should be concentrating on the lecturer.'

'Exactly, that is what makes me doze off, the concentration. I need something to distract me, which is absent in a classroom. Sometimes my brain goes blank, that is why I could not spell these words right. The lack of sleep is affecting my memory. Darling, it is hard. Very soon I will sit the first exam for this year, and I do not know what we have covered so far. The first two days of the week are manageable, but anything after is unbearable. I sometimes ask myself if it is worth going to lectures on Fridays. I honestly can't cope with Fridays anymore. So are the hours between three am and four at work. I languish in that period of the day probably because it is the time the whole city falls quiet. I worry that I may fail my exams this year. When I think about the struggle in the laboratory on Friday during the day and the prospect of putting my hand on something cold on the last coaches of inner-city trains at night, I feel like going back to the detention centre.'

'Oh no don't say things like that. Remember some people died there. Here is work and you are not going to die. I sympathise with you but don't compare labour to prison.'

'Very true, but over there, the worst that can happen to you aside from what you mentioned, and the deportation is cold showers in the morning, but if you remember your bloody ID number, you are fine. I can't skip a coach because of dumps and unclassified papers in the four corners of the coach. I cannot afford to miss a lesson either unless I accept defeat. So, what do I do? And then, when I think about what one of my fellow countrymen is going through, I believe we are both in hell. He does not have the proper papers to remain in this country. Each year he enrols on courses to be able to renew his student's visa. But to be able to do that, his bank account must be fat. He is in big trouble. He must undertake as many jobs as possible to be able to show an acceptable bank statement to the immigration. He is in the peregrination hoodwink. "God have mercy." That is why I am cross with African leaders. We may not have this standard of living, but I cannot see anyone suffering the way we do in this part of the world in Africa. The only trouble in Africa is politics. No one cleans somebody else's mess over there.'

JT never leaves the school building without saying goodbye to the receptionist. On one evening, the receptionist didn't hear from JT. She wonders whether JT had some issues or was still in the building. She asks the cleaner: 'Have you cleaned all the rooms?'

'No. I am waiting for the laboratory to be cleared. There seems to be one professor still working there. I knocked on the door and someone said to come in, but I thought I should let him finish his work. So, I said oh don't worry I will come back once you are finished.'

'Which professor? They have all signed off.'

'So, who is there then?'

JT frequently takes the back seat in the laboratory to avoid embarrassment in case he doses off. The receptionist and the cleaner, who desperately wants the laboratory free so that she can finish her work and go home, knock on the door, and hear once again 'come in'. They pushed the door and saw JT in a deep sleep. He felt a presence and jumped in embarrassment. The receptionist felt vindicated but also concerned. 'Don't you know that everyone is gone?' He then realised that he was not at home.

JT's prayer now was to finish his course and get out of the cleaning job. Benita felt the pain her husband was enduring. 'Darling, very soon it will be over,' she said. 'But when I compare your results from last year with what I am seeing now, I get seriously worried. I always said that your education was more important than any cleaning job now, although it helps you build your mother's house. Why don't you quit this job and concentrate on your studies?'

'I will think about it.'

CHAPTER 23

'Did I not vow to make life unbearable for this spurious fellow? He seemed to have settled comfortably well. How can I disturb his sleep now that he has fully conquered the heart and soul of Benita?' the war veteran was wondering. 'If I confront him, I will be in trouble with Benita, and she may not allow me to see my children. If I sit back and take no action, he will become the father of my children and I cannot live to see that. What is my best option?' KF brought the subject to the table in one of the conversations with his friend Ben and other war veterans.

'It is simple,' exclaims Ben.

'How?' KF asks.

'Set him up,' suggests Ben. 'Let me know when you are ready,' he adds.

'I am ready,' KF replies.

'Oh no, I need to prepare the trap properly otherwise we may be in trouble with the authorities. Do you know what he does?'

'I have no interest in what he does, why should I?'

'How are you going to get him if you do not have a clue what he does? What if he takes your children to Africa? You cannot invade his privacy when he is at home, your ex will defend him. If she sees you around her property, that may raise suspicions.'

'I see, what sort of time scale are we talking about?'

'The ball is in your court. You need to do your homework first. I need every single detail about him; when he goes out and when he comes in, whether he is studying or working, the name of the school, the workplace address …'

'Give me some time.'

'No worries, anytime.'

'Thank God it is Saturday today. At last, I am going to have some sleep. But first, I think, I will treat the children. It has been a while since we last visited the children's park. I believe they will be thrilled to hear the word "park" today. K has her favourite game there that is unfortunately not free. But it is not a big deal, since I get paid today, why not pamper the children? I just want to keep them happy. Their biological father would have done the same. They truly recognise me now as their father. So yes, later today we will play a little bit together before I go to sleep. Right now, what I need is two hours sleep before they get up and jump on me.' As JT walks past a wine bar, a seemingly drunk man stood in his way. 'Come and buy me a drink, my friend.'

'I don't drink,' JT answers.

'What do you mean you don't drink, are you not the man who took my bottle of wine two weeks ago?'

'You got the wrong man.'

'No, I got the right man. How many people look like you in this area?'

'Here we go again.' JT was thinking about what happened to him during his evasion from the detention centre. 'It is not me,' he replies. 'All I need now is my bed. I'm not interested in alcohol.'

'Are you saying that I am so drunk that I cannot recognise people?'

'I did not say you are buzzed.'

'Come on then, I know you. You are a gentleman.'

JT tried to avoid the man by moving to his right. The man also moves right. JT turned left the man did the same. JT recalled the experience he and Tcheba went through at the central coach station in Gadu. His heart started racing. He was thinking about what to do to avoid confrontation. 'Okay I will buy you a drink.' JT ordered a glass of beer for the man.

Behold, three men appear. 'What about us?' they ask.

'Oh no, I do not have money for that.'

'You have money, liar. You must also buy us a drink.'

'Okay, no problem.' JT moves to the counter and spots a second exit door. He pretends to order some beer pointing a finger at them. Before they know it, JT has vanished through the fire exit door. Unfortunately, the men quickly moved to the only exit to the street.

'You … we are going to teach you a lesson tonight. You should stay away from Benita or else you will meet us again.'

The three men kick JT from left to right. He drops his bag to defend himself. While JT was taking them down one by one, as a Shotokan black belt holder, one of them puts a large quantity of drugs in his bag. By the time the police reach the scene, the men have disappeared. The barman refuses to bear witness.

'Are you alright, sir?' the officers ask

'Yes, sirs,' he replies.

'So, what happened? Were you involved in heavy drinking?'

'No, I was coming from work.'

'Did you have a deal with them?'

'Which deal?' he asks.

'Drug deal.'

'No, I don't take drugs.'

'Can we search your bag?'

'Of course, you can,' JT did not have anything to hide.

The officers check his pockets first and then the bag. Behold three bags of white powder were revealed. 'What is this?' they ask.

'I don't know.'

'What do you call this? I thought you said you were coming from work.'

'I swear to God, I'm coming from work and there was nothing in that bag except for foodstuff.'

'Are you saying that someone else planted this in your bag? How can I believe you? Do not lie, tell me the truth.'

'I don't know. Maybe these drunkards did it.'

'I don't believe you. You are under arrest for drug possession.'

He wanted to call his family but that was not possible. He was worried sick for his wife and children. 'They must be panicking,' he thought.

'What is going on with this man again? Is he oversleeping somewhere on the site? By this time of the day, he should be having his breakfast and talking to the children.' Benita calls the workplace in a terrified voice.

'Sorry, madam, call after ten to speak with the night duty manager.'

'What? Why can't you tell me where my husband is now, and you want me to wait until night? I want to know now before it is too late.'

'Sorry, madam,' the man online said. 'This is a completely different team. We do not know what takes place at night. Sorry!'

Benita calls the local police station but there was no record in the name of Mr JT. He was picked up by a patrolling police unit that took him to a special station for notorious drug dealers. Benita thought that JT may have been involved in a road accident. 'Maybe he was too tired and could not watch for the traffic.' The night duty manager confirms that JT left the site at a quarter to five in the morning. Benita intensified her hospital search in vain. The local paper publishes pictures of a missing person as a thirty-two-year-old father of three and a nursing school student who has gone missing after a night shift at the eastern train depot. The special police station recognised the picture and contacted Benita. She races down to the prison.

'Darling, what happened? Are you alright?' she asks JT.

'I am okay, just worried for you and my future again. I may be deported if I stay here too long.'

'You will not be deported. Do not be negative. So, tell me the truth so that I know how to fight.'

'The truth is what you know. I think this is a setup, and my gut feeling is that it is your ex. He vowed to destroy my future.'

'I doubt it, my thoughts go to your thirty-year-old model.'

'Have I got a model? Why don't you trust me? If you believe I am still in touch with Dr Dami, you are deceiving yourself. I do not believe she would do anything like that. I do not think so. I honestly believe it is the work of KF. The men warned me to stay away from you.'

'So what? Your Dr Dami can give the same warning. The main point is for you to leave me.'

'You are right.'

'Listen, since I know the truth and your whereabouts, I must go back and start the process for getting you out. Please stay away from drug dealers. They may try to brainwash you. Be incredibly careful. Stay clean and you will be vindicated. Love you.'

JT was transferred to prison the following day after spending the night in a police cell. The officers believe he is a serious drug dealer and did not want to waste taxpayers' money by taking him to court. JT woke up the following morning in a familiar setting; bunkbed, calls for breakfast, roommates in a restricted environment... He believes he has been taken to a detention centre again. However, he notes that detainees here were different; they were aggressive. They do not dream about getting out soon, they confess their crimes. Some seem to be comfortable while others denounce injustice; they vow to clear their name once released. JT became confused. 'Is this a kind of nightmare or what? I remembered coming from work with plans for a family outing, only to find myself suddenly in prison. This can't be true; this is unreal.'

One month, two and three months passed, and JT still languishes behind bars for a crime he did not commit. Much as his account sounds credible, the legal system fails to establish a legal ground for a not-guilty verdict. He collapsed on the day he saw a uniform he recognises. The immigration officers came to remove some drug dealers. They called two names and took them outside. JT was very familiar with the practice. His roommate confirms that foreign inmates were regularly removed from prison for deportation. 'The government does not want to waste taxpayers' money on criminals. So, they send them back to their country of origins,' he concludes.

'Not again' JT thought. 'So, when am I going to be free in this country and do something? Am I going to spend my entire life on the hook of immigration? I can't prepare for my future, I can't look after Mum, I can't fight. What can I do? What am I allowed to do?' He cried in silence.

Benita was fully aware of the prospect of JT being deported should he spend more than eighteen months in prison as a foreigner. So, she decided to collect evidence and fight the case in court. She traced JT's itinerary from work, asking people around whether they witnessed any fight early in that morning. Her luck came when she bumped into someone at the wine bar where the action took place. The barman had only a faint recollection of what befell on that day. He nonetheless hinted that a conversation about who should strike first and who should put the drugs in the bag was heard. That was enough for Benita to make a case. Unfortunately, the court scheduled the hearing in six months, meaning that JT would have spent a total of twelve months in prison. That was risky. 'What if he does not win and I have to appeal? How long would it take?' Benita was thinking. 'This is not good enough. I need to get a good lawyer who can move the date forward.' Benita could no longer concentrate on her career. She wants to save her marriage first for her own sake and the sake of the children. She guesses that the children may have an unanswered question: 'Why is it that Daddy is always in prison?'

Benita ponders alone sitting at the dining table. 'What if JT is now involved in drug dealing? Has he given up the night job to do what can bring easy money? But this path is dangerous if this is his new career; cleaning jobs may be hard, but they are safe. Maybe the job is too much for him now as he complained about it in the past. Combining night duty with studies is demanding. So, where has he been spending nights then? Is he spending nights somewhere pretending he is going to work? Did he ask the manager to come up with some alibi should I call in? Who knows, he may be hiding something from me. I will confront him once he is out. How long has he been lying to me pretending he is going to work? I hope I am wrong. Maybe he is combining the two. However, if it turns out that he has been doing something behind my back, I ...'

One evening at the local bar where the vets go regularly for a glass of wine and to socialise, the 'boys' who did the dirty job for KF appear for their balance.

'What balance?' he asks.

'You did not pay the full amount for the job we did.'

'What job?' KF asks.

'You want to pay or not?'

'But I need to know the job you did for me first.'

'These are the men who set up your ex's husband. They are my boys. I paid them some money to do this job, do you think it was free? They put their lives at risk. The man could have had a knife or gun on him. I was supposed to pay the balance after they were finished, but you were nowhere to be found. So yes, five thousand SK is the outstanding balance,' Ben said.

'What? You're having a laugh. Who do you think I am? A charity that distributes free cash to drug addicts?' KF shot at Ben.

'Is this how you are going to pay me for helping you? You call me a drug addict?'

'Yes, you are. Did I ask you to hire men to confront that man I can take down myself with one finger?'

'When was the last time you looked at yourself in a mirror?'

'That is an insult, are you saying that I am too frail?'

'You said it. Looking at you the first thing that comes to my mind is where we are going to bury you.'

'I have had enough. I'm leaving. I do not want to send you to an emergency service. Nurses got better things to do.'

'You are going nowhere. You must pay the balance and now.'

'This is a rip off. You should have discussed it with me first. Where am I going to get five thousand SK? What sort of friend are you? You want to blackmail me and get some money for your hang-up?'

'Well, the drugs they put in his bag cost money. You must pay it back. The boys have been patient enough.'

'They can go to hell.'

'You want to pay now, or we will call the police and tell them the truth.'

'Go on, I am not interested. Did I go there to fight?'

The boys became agitated and close in on KF. One of the 'boys' put both of KF's hands in his left hand and stepped on KF's feet altogether. Ben tried to calm them down, but they were adamant. The barman, who did not want any trouble on his premises, calls the police who took away the group. Three days later, Benita received a phone call from the prison guard. 'Am I speaking with Mrs JT?'

'Yes, you are.'

'Ms Benita, I have some good news for you. Your man is waiting to be picked up. He is a free man.'

CHAPTER 24

'Now that the ordeal is over, we need to plan our future seriously. First, we will be going back to the town hall and this time, it must be big. You are now a citizen. No one can come and ask for your ID again. You are free, and no one can raise a finger to say … What? Why are you looking at me like that? Oh, I see, Dr Dami, right?'

'What does Dr Dami have to do with our wedding?'

'So why do you look at me funny as soon as I said that no one can raise a finger?'

'What do you mean I look funny? Don't you know that I have a funny face?'

'So, you have a funny face today, right? Who told the Ministry of Interior that we were getting married? How do they know?'

'How am I supposed to know? It could be your ex. He vowed that my dream would be shattered. My suspicion is on him.'

'I see, anyway, we are free this time to celebrate our union. Second, we need to rebuild your mum's house. It does not cost that much so that we can spend our summer holidays with her. I have never been to Africa, and this could be an opportunity to discover the continent. I'm sure the kids will love it. They would like to see the monkeys, elephants and giraffes.'

'Monkeys, certainly yes, but no giraffe. There is no giraffe in West Africa. We will have to travel to the East to see the elephants and giraffes. You can find some elephants in West Africa, sure.'

'You don't seem enthusiastic. What is going on in your mind?'

'What makes you say that? Are you now a psychologist?'

'Here we go, I knew your mind was on your "psychologist". No wonder why your answers are short.'

'Don't get me wrong, darling. You should know that I adore you. I was just taking mental notes. That is why you think I am being short in my responses.'

'I love you too. So, thirdly, and the most important part, guess what, we will soon be rich.'

'How?' JT asks with excitement.

'You see, your voice and face have changed at hearing of money.'

'Of course, being rich is what I long for. I work hard to live a good life.'

'I don't blame you. You deserve a better life. You would have qualified as a medical doctor long ago, I guess, had you not lost your ID. But it is better late than never.'

'Yes, and a "big man" over there with maids and perhaps a chauffeur to drop my children to school.'

'It's not late yet. Anyway, first, the insurance claim for your accident. That mad driver nearly killed you. You must be compensated for your injuries and the cost of rehabilitation.'

'What sort of money are we talking about?'

'Almost six figures, I suspect.'

'What? That's serious money.'

'Of course! Secondly, compensation for the injuries you sustained during the deportation fight. Remember the security guards nearly broke your arms at the airport. Third, the compensation for trauma and anxiety when the fire broke out at the detention centre and the treatment you were subjected to.'

'Oh, not that one, it was our fault. We deliberately set the centre ablaze to escape. We should take full responsibility for that.'

'Well, would you have done that had the living conditions been appropriate?'

'No.'

'So, that is it. Now I cannot remember where I was with my explanation.'

'You were talking about compensation and that they put my life at risk.'

'Yes, that is it. And we will sue the Ministry of Immigration for disrupting our wedding. They will reimburse all the money I put into the organisation. I warned them that they would pay for their blunder. I will fight my case, but also to save future marriages. It is sickening to ruin someone's special day like that. I believe, after all this, we will be in the money. We will have a decent marriage. And we can have some left over after the wedding to move to a posh area and if possible, set up a business. So, let us celebrate our victory with champagne.'

'You did not mention private schools for our children.'

'It is not a must in this country, state schools are equally good as private schools.'

'And Africa?'

'I am not sure about living in Africa. Holidays in Africa, yes, but to live there permanently, I am not sure yet. Maybe after the children have grown up. I would not put the future of my children at risk. I don't think schools over there are well equipped to prepare children for today's challenges.'

'Right, I take your point. Now that I am free to do what is legally possible, with your favour, there are three areas that I intend to investigate: first, I intend to organise my fellow Africans. I would like to set up a foundation that will not only cater for the welfare of former students whose legal status in this country is uncertain but will help them fully integrate into this society and contribute to the advancement of citizenship.

The second thing is a lobbying group to bring about changes in Africa. I cannot live to see the suffering of my people all the time and no lesson is learnt. I will gather some good and like-minded guys to work on the project. The person I have in mind is Zokoh, who now works for a local bank. I will then contact the fellow professor from a neighbouring country who has converted his African qualifications and is lecturing at one of the universities in Bezalazur. I could envisage five members for the time being: Zokoh, Yessy, the professor from Asunite, Mapu, a medical doctor from Maputa and Setty, a lawyer from another neighbouring country. The group will not only put pressure on African leaders to be more accountable for their actions and fight against corruption but reward good governance. Each year, the group will organise a reward ceremony for the African head of state who has met all the indicators of good governance and importantly has made great progress around freedoms. The group will debate on development and international relations. Group members will frequently travel to Africa to assess the impact of their actions.'

'With your permission, can I make some suggestions?'

'Of course, you are more than welcome.'

'I personally believe that your priority should be dealing with the "blame culture" in your community.'

'What do you mean?'

'I have noticed the lack of responsibility by your people. Although I sympathise with those who have suffered under the asylum system in this country, the short time I have spent with you and your fellow Africans has taught me one single lesson. Your people don't fight for a cause. They run away from a brutal regime, they run away from corruption, they run away from poverty. How are we going to benefit from the good weather in Africa if conditions are not improved? Whatever happened to them is someone else's fault. It is other people who make them do what they do or become who they are today. For me, without a cultural shift, I doubt your lobbying group could achieve its noble goal. Let me tell you something, how did this place get rid of dictatorship, kingship, and other restrictions? Did you think you could have the freedom we enjoy today without putting up a fight? But your people say that other people impose a leader over them. They say that other countries exploit their natural resources. They say they are poor because others did not transfer their technologies to them. What sort of mentality is that? Do they want to do nothing and expect others to grant them their heart's desires? Can they not create like others? What stops them? They say that they do not have the resources, but I heard that some men in Africa can be as wealthy as some nations in the world. The leaders loot their own resources and stock them somewhere for someone else to benefit. That is madness. And you people are aware of this and take no action except to moan. So, what's wrong with your people? If your people stop blaming history, they will stand the chance of facing the future. If they stop blaming others, they will stand the chance of fighting for a better future. Until then, I can only be sorry for you. Being colonised is not an issue but failing to take your destiny into your own hands is a tragedy. Being poor is not an issue but failing to change the course of life is suicidal. You were colonised because you were weak, but what are you doing to avoid further colonisation? I am not a historian, but this is what history taught me. In 1848, there was a revolution known in some countries as the "Springtime of the Peoples" or the "Springtime of Nations". The revolution was born from some disruptive ideas such as democracy, liberalism, radicalism, nationalism, and socialism because of widespread dissatisfaction with political leadership. In the language of the 1840s, "democracy" meant replacing an electorate of property-owners with universal male suffrage, while "Liberalism" referred to the consent of the governed, restriction of church and state power, republican government, freedom of the press and the individual. "Nationalism" on the other hand believed in uniting people bound by some mix of common languages, culture, religion, shared history, and immediate geography. This is what history said. But the people did not simply develop ideas and expect others to make them come to fruition. They fought for it. The revolutions suffered a series of defeats in the summer of 1849 and tens of thousands of people were killed, and many more were forced into exile. But some social reforms proved permanent, and years later nationalists gained their objectives. The problem is that your people have no idea how to defend nor the guts to fight for a cause. How can you bring about a change if everyone is ready to run away at the hearing of a rumour? Your people are dominated by fear and emotion. You cannot build anything on emotion or fear. By the way, the brutal regime gave me a man I love, so it's not all bad.'

'You have caught me on the back foot. I think I need to sleep on this. I can see myself in this equation. I never realised that we were so dependent on other people. I knew that in my culture, peoples' opinions count more in our decision-making, and sometimes we prefer that people decide for us so that we do not become subject to criticism, but your remark is so pertinent that I need time to come back to you.'

CHAPTER 25

The second-year results were so poor that Benita insisted JT drop the night job to concentrate on his studies. He did so well in his third year that the school advised him to consider a different path to qualify as a medical doctor.

'Are you aware of the conversion course for practising nurses to pursue their medical studies?' they ask JT.

'No, I have no idea,' he answers.

'Well, with your four years of medical studies in your country, and three years of nursing studies, and looking at your scores this year, I do not doubt that you can achieve this goal. Would you like us to recommend you? This means three more years of studies if you do not mind.'

'That would be a dream come true. Thanks in advance.'

'I had never thought that this could be possible. This would be unthinkable had I remained in Africa.' He got home with a big smile that exposed the big gap between his teeth.

'What is the good news?' Benita probed.

The school wonders whether I could take the next step to qualify as a medical doctor.

'That is good news. Is it not what you always wanted? I'm glad to hear that, but darling, this is a long way to go; six to seven years.'

'No, two to three years that will take. They will consider my past studies.'

'Go for it then. What are you waiting for?'

'I needed to share with you first.'

'You don't need to share things like that with me, go on.'

'Thanks for your support.'

JT suddenly became sad. 'What's the matter?' Benita asks. 'You must be grateful to God and cheerful.'

'How can I possibly be? This qualification come too late, five years late. I could have behind me five years' experience as a medical doctor and decent savings had the immigration service not kept me unnecessarily in detention. I have lost huge earnings. I am grateful to this country but angry at the same time. I am also quiet because I am very far away from my mum. How is she going to benefit from my success? She may hear that I am doing well, but how can she be sure that people are not lying to her? And had I been in my country, I would be visiting her regularly in the village and taking care of her. Right now, I don't know if she is eating well or in good health. And she would be also expecting to see me every month had I been there. Seeing me will give her joy and long life. She can't see me nor touch me. I know she must be very worried. I'm sure she is still wondering whether I eat my favourite sauce. And she does not know her grandchildren nor can she talk to them; she only speaks our language. You see, right now, my mind is going through all the traumas I went through.'

'Please, get over it! What's done is done and there is nothing you can do about it.'

'Right, who wants to see Africa?'

'Me,' the children answered, except for the youngest who did not know what they were talking about.

'What would you like to see in Africa?'

'Elephants, giraffes and snakes?'

'Snakes?'

'Yes?'

'Well, you will see many, but they are dangerous. They can kill people. If you see a snake in Africa, please call Mummy or Daddy. Do not play with them. You do not want to see Grandmama?

'We want to see Grandmama. Has she got a Tele?' they ask.

'There is no Tele in the village but there is something that replaces it. I'm sure you will like it. If you see it, you will forget about Tele, but I'm not going to tell you now. I will keep it as a secret until we are ready to go, maybe next year.'

'That's not fair,' they said.

'Life is not fair, children. We need to prepare for the trip properly. We will need to buy as many light T-shirts, shorts, hats, and sandals as we can. It is hot in Africa, and you cannot wear what you have got now. So, think about what you want Daddy to buy for you. Think about the colour and let Daddy know, okay?'

'What is there in the village for me?' Benita wonders. 'All I have heard is mosquitos, hunger and bad roads.'

'What you heard is the view of my friend Tcheba. He did not grow up in the village and did not have any other friends in the village. Life in the village could be sweet. There is always night entertainment by villagers at full moon. The other thing I enjoy in village life is sharing food. People sit in a big circle around five pm and women bring food. This is not about family, but neighbours; about two to three households get together and share their food. Men use the opportunity to chat but also deal with certain marital issues they do not want to take to the village chief. In those cases, this is what I observed, men use codes so that the children do not follow the conversation. In one of their conversations, a man complained that his wife had not served him water to bathe for about a week. So, he had not had his bath for about a week. I nearly said that he was lying because I saw the woman taking a bucket of warm water to the shower place the day before. But as I became an adult, I believe they were not talking about the actual shower. I like the community spirit in the village. Farming is done in groups in rotation; about seven men get together and spend a day on each member's farm. They tell stories while working. So, you do not feel the pain of hard labour. Marvellous things take place in the village. Once, I experienced this myself. As we were working in a group on a member's farm, around two pm, the sky turned dark. Heavy rain was about to fall. One of the men went into the bush and sat down by a tall tree. He sent out a warning sound three times, then he went silent. Heavy rain fell around the farm, while the farm itself remained dry. We continued our work undisturbed. After half an hour, the rain stops. Then the man emerged to the amazement of the group. I must admit that I did not work during the thirty minutes the rainfall lasted. How did he do it? I was asking myself.

He knew that I was confused. He looked at me and smiled. I have many more stories like these but do not want to bore you. They taught me wisdom. Great! I think you were right; we need a break; you look exhausted. You have been my rock. You received more bullets from the Ministry of Interior than I did. Where are we heading to?'

'Just pack your suitcase,' Benita suggests.

JT must learn to reconcile two different cultures, and there is no doubt he often falls short in recognising some European values. He often fails to offer Benita flowers when it matters. He does not write birthday or some memorable occasion cards. He believes that Benita knows that he loves her with ALL his heart. Although Benita understands, she sometimes felt disappointed; perhaps JT does not love her that much anymore. JT always promises to learn and do better next time.

Benita also recognises her weakness; there are some aspects of the African culture that she does not master. 'Naturally, there are certain things dear to my husband that I cannot offer because I simply do not know. JT sometimes misses his traditional food. He wishes he could cook it himself as I do not have any idea how to nail the various ingredients for a delicious taste. The first time I tried to cook the okra sauce was a disaster and since then, I rebuff further embarrassment. African cuisine is time-consuming.'

As time goes on JT begins to dream about his long spell at Camp X. Benita woke up to a loud laugh. 'Got you, I am not going to miss my breakfast anymore. I know my ID. CX1752005, correct?'

'What is he saying?' Benita murmurs. She looks into JT's eyes, but he was sleeping. She lies down again and sleeps. Another night, she woke up to the same number reading. So, she wondered what could be going on. The following morning, she read back the numbers to JT.

'How do you know these numbers,' he asks.

'You have been recently disturbing my sleep with loud laughter and these numbers,' she says. 'And this happens around three am.'

'Aha, this is my ID number in Camp X. If you recall, I described to you our nights in Camp X.'

'Should we call the psychiatrist? He may advise us.'

'Oh no, no need. I will be alright.'

'Darling, do you not think your fellow Africans may be suffering from PTSD?'

'What is PTSD again?' JT asks.

'Post-traumatic stress disorder. Remember, I asked you to see a psychiatrist?'

'What has this got to do with me? I told you that these people refuse to look after themselves and always make poor decisions.'

'Just for you to understand my point.'

'I know, but there is nothing wrong with me. Furthermore, I do not want you to complain that I am developing a close relationship with a psychiatrist.'

'Do not worry, it will not be a female this time, no way. You see the way your people behave could be the consequence of the way they were welcomed in this country. You may think that they have lived here long enough to behave like the natives. However, at the back of their mind, they carry the scars of immigration. The humiliation and frustration they were once upon a time subject to may remain present in their mind, and therefore they can struggle to make the right decision sometimes. You argue that some Africans brought with them luggage that keeps them in poverty, the truth is that many believe that they still face detention and deportation. My understanding is that they may not feel welcome given the treatment they received in detention centres. And for young people who leave their country for the very first time, the experience is agonising. Thus, in their mind they believe the host country does not want them, that is why they treat them like criminals, and this follows them their entire life. I have always been here to fight for you, but those people may not have anyone to rely on when they face deportation. I think it is for this reason you collect money to bail out some members, am I correct?'

'Yes, you are. You got a point. I am listening.'

'Even though they have been granted the right to remain,' she continues, 'they believe they do not have the same equal rights as the natives, since they could be deported should they misbehave or find themselves in the wrong place at the wrong time. Remember I was running against the clock the time you were in prison to avoid you spending more than eighteen months in there.'

'That is again correct and scary.'

'Now you understand why they may become reluctant to

participate in certain activities of life over here. They may become too cautious and fail to express themselves or fully utilise their talents. They may convince themselves they are looked on as foreigners or visitors. In this case, they refuse to be fully involved in what will affect their welfare. Others may involuntarily segregate themselves by living in groups and certain areas. Together, they feel strong.'

'Not quite right, a bunch of sheep will never turn into a lion. I think they should mingle with the natives. They keep themselves apart, fearing rejection from the natives, I know. But this is the wrong attitude to assume that everyone behaves the same. Nevertheless, you are right, I sometimes feel angry, disenchanted, and frightened. I suppose Tetnov lives by human rights; however, this does not apply to outsiders and those seeking to enter the country, I believe. But it does not mean that they will live their entire life in a "cage". They must learn to live with the trauma.'

'I'm without doubt that former detainees including yourself should be entitled to free counselling to recover their full sense to live a normal life in this society. Otherwise, they will remain a "second-class citizen" and never fully contribute to this great nation.'

CHAPTER 26

'Do eagles not fly high and alone with eagles? Eagles soar in the sky to separate themselves from mingling with other birds and be in a class of their own.' JT strongly believes that to excel he must move away from time wasters and those who keep looking backwards. Thus, moving away from the African community could be his best course of action. However, his views are echoed with scepticism. Benita has always enjoyed the exuberance that he brings home after his community association's meetings. 'It is good to see this man with a smile on his face, this lightens our relationship. I know my weakness and this association can be vital to our union', Benita was thinking, acknowledging cultural differences. Thus, Benita was confused at the announcement that he is turning his back on the organisation that helped him in his early days. 'Did you not say that you enjoy your meetings because you can share your traditional meals?' Benita asks.

'Yes, I did, but the way things are moving, I believe by remaining in the group I may end up being like the other members.'

'What do you mean?' Benita queries, thinking they were involved in dodgy businesses.

'Well, all the talks at the meetings are around Africa, which is understandable. However, in the long run, we may not have any plan for our old days in this country. And that is what is intriguing me.'

'Did you ask them about their plans for this country?'

'No, it did not cross my mind.'

'You should, otherwise, you will not have been of any good to them. Maybe they need someone to remind them or direct them.'

JT believes Benita has a point. If he does not advise or try to remind them about what made them come here in the first place, then he will not have contributed to the group. He works out how to approach the subject. 'I am always puzzled to listen to these people. I wonder what happened to their dreams, desires to go back to our country and bring about changes. I share their passion for Kombi; however, I can't see any clear plan for a foreseeable return. For the few who are unclear about their future move, I can't see either how they are preparing for their stay. It seems that as they age, the flame in them dims. Yet, I sense they must have high IQs, no doubt. And to imagine they suffered like I did to enter this country and surrender all the hope for a better life is pathetic. Should I ask them? I guess a couple of things happened to them, and these are just my conclusions from the chats with some members, don't get me wrong.

First, bad politics in Africa deters them from returning home. High corruption and a volatile atmosphere due to civil unrest mean that there is little prospect for a brighter future with their European qualifications and therefore they resolve to remain in Europe.

The second element of the argument is the reality of

Western civilisation. In this society, it is individualism. It is "make or break". You work hard, you enjoy the fruit of your labour. There is no one to pull the strings for you. The absence of corruption means that people deserve their position. So, when they get their back against the wall here, the next option offered to them is to look back to Africa. At least Africa is the devil they know well.

So how do you convince them that home is here if they cannot see themselves as part of this society? Equally, how do you encourage them to return home in good time if they see little prospect of fulfilment in their homeland? Which of these two lands can serve them best? How can I possibly assist them in making the right decision? Should I assist or leave?'

'May I remind you about a story you told me in the past.'

'Which story?'

'The story of twelve Africans that went home to meet a government official.'

'Thank you, Benita. This is a story one of the members of our community association told us at a meeting. He said, upon taking power in Maputa, General K dreamed about a government of excellence. He was seeking academics and great leaders to be at the heart of his administration. He wanted intellectuals with a vision of a better Africa to edge competition with neighbouring countries. He sent his minister for labour to hunt for talents in the diaspora. The man was overwhelmed by the hospitality of the African community in Bezalazur. After the meal and some performances by African artists, he announced the purpose of his visit. He set a timetable for those who were willing to help their country. "We want those who are patriotic. We want to fulfil some positions at the ministry for science and education, development, new technology, planning and international relationship... All you need to do is to compile your CV and see me. I will then direct you myself to relevant departments. We urgently need people like you, Africa needs people like you." That is what he told those that attended the reception. It was an era of local rivalry in Africa. Each state wanted to boast about the level of education in the country by filling their administration with highly educated personnel (this is no longer the case). Twelve Bengis decided to return home and help their continent. They were welcomed by their respective families. They informed their families about their imminent appointment as ministers. The team went to meet Prof Dee Folg on the appointed day. The minister, as promised, sacrificed one day of his precious time to appoint the right person to the right post. He had promised his colleagues ministers that he was recruiting specialists in various subjects from well-trusted universities in the West under the recommendation of the head of the state. On the day he took the first CV that read in its profile: "Fifteen years of experience at the National bank." The minister got excited. "We have people like these, and our banking system is collapsing." However, what he saw in the job description shocked him; cleaning the reception area at the bank, cleaning the toilets...He put the CV on the side. The second CV was for a care assistant without proper medical knowledge. The CV holder could administer medication to patients but under supervision. He put the CV aside. The next one was for someone in his early fifties with over twenty years of experience cleaning trains at the central train depot. The minister was getting confused and nervous. He grabbed another one hoping to find something different. "Yes, now we are talking". He got the CV of someone with years' experience working at the central hospital in the capital. The owner had previously worked for one of the top hotel chains in the country. "Aren't we getting there? Our tourism sector is dying. This man may help". The minister was curious to read under his specific role. The man has been working for the hospital chain as a chambermaid. It was the same duty he was performing for the hospital. The minister diplomatically concealed his anger and advised the men to bring their passports the following day for some paperwork and employment contracts. The Bengis were excited at the prospect of getting a ministerial position bar one of them that had a negative feeling. "But the minister did not give any clue about our appointment, that is strange", he said. But the group accused him of being negative. The following morning, the minister split the group in two, one was sent to clean the central hospital and the other to clean the national prison. He made sure that they did not escape by giving them free accommodation and transport. At six in the morning, the driver was there to pick them up. The Bengis were visibly terrified and felt betrayed. They believed the minister had paid the hospitality he received in Tetnov with punishment. After two weeks of work without proper wages, the minister called them to his office and asked them if they were enjoying their positions. They all went quiet with shame. They all became small in their own eyes having been humiliated.

'Right', the minister said, 'I treated you harshly because I believe you were taking me for a fool. Seriously, is it this that you have been doing all along in Europe? We need your expertise to advance our nation. What you have seen over there, many over here long to see. Science, technological advances, and good governance are what we are after, and you have the privilege to live in those developed countries to just dwell in cleaning jobs? You are lucky guys. I was impressed and jealous at the same time when I visited you there. Now, I may be drawing a wrong conclusion, perhaps you do not want to stay here. Otherwise, would I have a different CV from you please?'

The men confessed to the minister that they had always been doing cleaning jobs to support themselves and their families. 'Cleaning jobs are not part-time jobs to sustain you while you study?' the minister question. Why did you dwell in part-time jobs? Does the system prevent you from accessing professional bodies? If you spend your time doing cleaning jobs, how good would you be to our country and continent? We rely on your knowledge for the future of this continent, but you are not far from a disgrace. You let yourself, your family, and your country down. I do not believe that in future we will dream about recruiting from the diaspora. Potential seas have turned into brooks. You can collect your passport at the reception and decide whether to continue your cleaning jobs here or abroad." This incident has caused us to close the doors to any further diaspora recruitment project.'

CHAPTER 27

Three years after Benita and JT sealed their relationship before God and man, the Africans in exile continue to comment on the wedding reception. 'This man must have money,' some people say. 'Oh no, it is the wife that is wealthy,' others argue.

'It doesn't matter whether it is the wife or the man, the bottom line is that they had the most extravagant and memorable wedding our community has experienced in this land,' another man says.

'Unlike us, JT is more organised; he never talked about sending money home every day. I believe he planned this wedding well in advance. What I most liked about the wedding reception is the order and the way they served the food. There were no complaints, no fights over seat location. Wherever your seat was, you had a good view of the high table. By the way, what is happening with JT? I haven't seen him recently,' the man wonders.

'Don't mind him. Like Zokoh, I believe he is leaving us,' the man nicknamed 'Dr' says. 'You may have noticed his recent comments. He even tried to dissuade me from sending money home. He complained that we waste more money on Africa than on ourselves. He said this place is our new home, that we should rethink our lifestyle, that we should think about our living conditions first before sending all our hard-earned money to relatives in Africa. I told him that he had not understood the greater cause. We are not here to become MILLIONAIRES; that would be selfishness. We are lucky to have made it, but how much more are those suffering in Africa, so me, Dr, I will continue to send money so that people do not mock my family.'

'Who told you that people are suffering in Africa? When was the last time you went to Africa?' a woman nicknamed Kakato reacts angrily. 'You people deceive yourselves here. I went to Kombi last year and felt sorry for myself when I saw one of my old friends over there, in the diamond business. She took me to her mansion in one of the trendiest areas of Gadu. I asked myself what I was doing here. I felt ashamed. So please do not put everyone in Africa in one basket. My friend has two maids, two drivers, two cooks, one to cook African food, the other European meals, although she has never been to Europe. Since then, I only send money when it is necessary and especially for children's school fees and medical bills, anything else I am not interested in. Each month we come here, eat and drink and nothing else. There is nothing on our agenda that could serve to prepare for our retirement nor change our living conditions in this great city. We live in poor conditions in government houses. Tell me, who does not have at least two jobs here? How many of us are still studying? You call yourself "doctor", did you not drop your architecture course five years ago, having gone halfway? We should be in the money for the effort we put into work, but we have nothing to show for it. Don't fool yourself. And you know what? JT and his wife have bought a new house, a four-bed house in Amian.'

'Really?' acknowledges another man in amazement. 'No wonder! I see … Well, we need to do something for this group,' the man continues. 'I know what we are going to do this coming summer. Together, we are going to audit our assets in Kombi. We may not have anything in this country, but we are somebody back home. I have made my parents build a mansion for me in our village and you people have done the same. Semy – one of the members – has a transport business, my friend over there, with grey hair and another colour that I am struggling to describe, owns a farming business, am I right?' They respond yes together and laugh about the description of the man's hair.

Seven men in total decided to make that trip. The women were unimpressed with the idea that could be seen as showing off. 'We should not embarrass ourselves, hearing Kakato's story,' the women were thinking. The men went and on the second night organised a big party in one of the most popular wine bars in the capital. 'The Gadu people must know that the boys are in town.' They blew all their money on young women and men they did not know. The locals call them the 'Bengis' and they were happy. The following day, they travelled to their counties of origin to evaluate their investments. They received a hero's welcome in their respective towns and villages. The next day, they asked their relatives to take them on a tour of their investments. Instead, they were asked to take their time and be received by those who have not seen them for ages. The men became impatient when they discovered their relatives were trying to buy time as they were not expecting them to return. Those who oversaw the house building and transport business vanished on the second day of the men's visit. The men suspected something was not right. They began to exercise pressure on those who were around them as family members. They were shocked to note that there was no mansion built in their name as the parents claimed when they sent fake pictures to hide the mismanagement of the money they received, transport business, or industrial farming business. In disbelief and bitterness, the men cursed their relatives and vowed never to see them again. They rushed back to Gadu and shortened their stay.

Back in Bezalazur, they did not know what to tell the women, nor their next move. Some of the men borrowed money from the bank to fulfil the historic trip of the 'Seven'. Others were left with no money to face their financial obligations. Their living conditions deteriorated; they borrowed more money to fix their financial shortfalls and buried their heads in several jobs to make ends meet. Doctor tried as much as he could to avoid Kakato. 'Perhaps JT was right and Kakato was right too,' they were thinking. But they did not want anyone to hear about their misadventure. They wished it were a nightmare.

'So, these people take us for idiots, *hein*? You kill yourself in this cold weather here for them to have the cream. At least they could make good use of the little money we send for their own sake, and then for our retirement, but there is nothing there and nothing here either and we are getting older and weak. How can we go back if there is no place for us to lay our heads? No savings, no business, no house, what a waste?'

CHAPTER 28

'Now that I'm a qualified medical doctor and have my own property in a good area in the capital, I wonder whether opening up a clinic that could ease pressure on hospitals could be enough as a contribution for the support I received in my time of struggle. I was fortunate to benefit from the support of strangers and a social system that helped me rescue my career. As I reflect on my journey full of push and pull, I wonder whether I could be who I am today had it not been for the support of this community. Many people sadly miss their goal in life simply because they could not meet a helpful hand at a crucial time.

I'm not sure that providing free medical consultation would be enough as a return on these people's investment in my becoming who I am today. But for the time being, I think this is what I can offer. Perhaps I could move into politics to defend the cause of my people in future. The danger is, with politics things can go out of control and the people you were trying to help can turn against you. When it happens, what do I become? A candidate for detention again? Is that what I want? I don't think I would like to go down that route again. I want to help, but life in detention is not what I long to live for again. I understand why those who become citizens after a long battle with immigration never fully contribute to this society. They become too cautious and fail to express themselves or fully utilise their talents. Like my people, I will do what I can without attracting the attention of authorities. I will limit my involvement in certain activities, including politics. I don't think I have the same equal rights as the natives. I am only a second-class citizen, the '*other citizen*', the outsider. For the sake of my children and wife that fought for my freedom all around, I will stay away from some activities. I know I could do more, but I must be careful; that's called wisdom. If I put my neck out there and anything goes wrong, the entire family will be the loser. I recall my second spell in detention, it was more painful than the first one when I did not know really what was going on; to be separated from family is agonising. I remember Benita running back and forth like a ping-pong ball so that I did not spend more than eighteen months in prison and qualify for deportation under immigration law. So, despite paying back my dues and gaining citizenship, I am still in the nest of immigration and the outsider.'

Brush Oulai is a critic and philosopher who believes the world could be a better place if people were given freedom to develop. He questions the good intention of world leaders and the politics of power to oppress the weak.

Mr Oulai is a journalist, songwriter, musician, and businessman. He graduated from the University of North London in business studies. He completed his MBA Finance at Oxford Brooks University. He holds an MSc Purchasing and Supply Chain Management from Robert Gordon University in Aberdeen, Scotland. He lives in Welling, Kent with his wife Rose and two lovely daughters, Taddy and Deslay.